The
Summer
of the Swans

BETSY BYARS

HAMPTON-BROWN

THE EXCHANGE

**When do
you really
know someone?**

Hampton-Brown
P.O. Box 223220
Carmel, California 93922
800-333-3510
www.hampton-brown.com

Printed in the United States of America

ISBN 0-7362-2808-X

05 06 07 08 09 10 11 12 13 14 10 9 8 7 6 5 4 3 2 1

The Summer of the Swans

Sara is having a terrible summer. Sometimes she feels happy, but then she feels sad. Sara talks with her sister, Wanda. Then she goes to sit with her little brother, Charlie.

Chapter One

Sara Godfrey was lying on the bed tying a kerchief on the dog, Boysie. "Hold your chin up, Boysie, will you?" she said as she braced herself on one elbow. The dog was old, slept all the time, and he was lying on his side with his eyes closed while she lifted his head and tied the scarf.

Her sister Wanda was sitting at the dressing table combing her hair. Wanda said, **"Why don't you leave Boysie alone?"**

"There's nothing else to do," Sara answered without looking up. "You want to see a show?"

"Not particularly."

"It's called 'The Many Faces of Boysie.'"

"Now I know I don't want to see it."

....

Why don't you leave Boysie alone? Stop bothering the dog.
"Not particularly." "No, not really."

Sara held up the dog with the kerchief neatly tied beneath his chin and said, "The first face of Boysie, proudly presented for your entertainment and amusement, is the Russian Peasant Woman. Taaaaaa-daaaaaa!"

"Leave the dog alone."

"He likes to be in shows, don't you, Boysie?" She untied the scarf, refolded it and set it carefully on top of the dog's head. "And now for the second face of Boysie, we travel halfway around the world to the mysterious East, where we see Boysie the **Inscrutable** Hindu. Taaaaaaa-daaaaaa!"

With a sigh Wanda turned and looked at the dog. "That's pathetic. In people's age that dog is eighty-four years old." She shook a can of hair spray and sprayed her hair. "And besides, that's my good scarf."

"Oh, all right." Sara fell back heavily against the pillow. **"I can't do anything around here."**

"Well, if it's going to make you that miserable, I'll watch the show."

"I don't want to do it any more. It's no fun now. This place smells like **a perfume factory.**" She put the scarf over

....

Inscrutable Mysterious

"I can't do anything around here." "I do not get to have fun."

a perfume factory you sprayed perfume all over it

her face and stared up through the thin blue material. Beside her, Boysie lay back down and curled himself into a ball. They lay without moving for a moment and then Sara sat up on the bed and looked down at her long, lanky legs. She said, "I have the biggest feet in my school."

"Honestly, Sara, I hope you are not going to start listing all the millions of things wrong with you because I just don't want to hear it again."

"Well, it's the truth about my feet. One time in **Phys Ed** the boys started throwing the girls' sneakers around and Bull Durham got my sneakers and put them on and they fit perfectly! How do you think it feels to wear the same size shoe as Bull Durham?"

"People don't notice things like that."

"Huh!"

"No, they don't. I have **perfectly terrible** hands—look at my fingers—only I don't **go around all the time saying,** 'Everybody, look at my stubby fingers, I have stubby fingers, everybody,' to *make* people notice. You should just ignore things that are wrong with you. The truth is everyone else is so worried about what's wrong with *them* that—"

....

Phys Ed gym class
perfectly terrible ugly
go around all the time saying always tell people

"It is very difficult to ignore the fact that you have huge feet when Bull Durham is dancing all over the gym in your shoes. They were not stretched the tiniest little bit when he took them off either."

"You wear the same size shoe as **Jackie Kennedy Onassis** if that makes you feel any better."

"How do you know?"

"Because one time when she was going into an Indian temple she had to leave her shoes outside and some reporter looked in them to see what size they were." She leaned close to the mirror and looked at her teeth.

"Her feet *look* littler."

"That's because she doesn't wear orange sneakers."

"I like my orange sneakers." Sara sat on the edge of the bed, slipped her feet into the shoes, and held them up. "What's wrong with them?"

"Nothing, except that when you want to hide something, you don't go painting it orange. I've got to go. Frank's coming."

She went out the door and Sara could hear her crossing into the kitchen. Sara lay back on the bed, her head next to Boysie. She looked at the sleeping dog, then

....

Jackie Kennedy Onassis a former first lady of the United States covered her face with her hands and began to cry noisily.

"Oh, Boysie, Boysie, I'm crying," she wailed. Years ago, when Boysie was a young dog, he **could not bear** to hear anyone cry. Sara had only to pretend she was crying and Boysie would come running. He would whine and dig at her with his paws and lick her hands until she stopped. Now he lay with his eyes closed.

"Boysie, I'm crying," she said again. "I'm really crying this time. Boysie doesn't love me."

The dog shifted uneasily without opening his eyes.

"Boysie, Boysie, I'm crying, I'm so sad, Boysie," she wailed, then stopped and sat up abruptly. "You don't care about anybody, do you, Boysie? A person could **cry herself to death** these days and you wouldn't care."

She got up and left the room. In the hall she heard the tapping noise of Boysie's feet behind her and she said without looking at him, "I don't want you now, Boysie. Go on back in the bedroom. Go on." She went a few steps farther and, when he continued to follow her, turned and looked at him. "In case you are confused, Boysie, a dog is supposed to comfort people and run up and nuzzle them and make them feel better. All you want to do is lie on soft

....

could not bear did not like
cry herself to death cry forever

things and hide bones in the house because you are too lazy to go outside. Just go on back in the bedroom."

She started into the kitchen, still followed by Boysie, who could not bear to be left alone, then heard her aunt and Wanda arguing, **changed her mind**, and went out onto the porch.

Behind her, Boysie scratched at the door and she let him out. "Now quit following me."

Her brother Charlie was sitting on the top step and Sara sat down beside him. She held out her feet, looked at them, and said, "I like my orange sneakers, don't you, Charlie?"

He did not answer. He had been eating a lollipop and the stick had come off and now he was trying to put it back into the red candy. He had been trying for so long that the stick was bent.

"Here," she said, "I'll do it for you." She put the stick in and handed it to him. "Now be careful with it."

She sat without speaking for a moment, then she looked down at her feet and said, "I hate these orange sneakers. I just *hate* them." She leaned back against the porch railing so she wouldn't have to see them and said,

....

changed her mind decided not to go in

"Charlie, I'll tell you something. This has been the worst summer of my life."

She did not know exactly why this was true. She was doing the same things she had done last summer—walk to the Dairy Queen with her friend Mary, baby-sit for Mrs. Hodges, watch television—and yet everything was different. It was as if her life was a huge **kaleidoscope**, and the kaleidoscope had been turned and now everything was changed. The same stones, shaken, no longer made the same design.

But it was not only one different design, one change; **it was a hundred**. **She could never be really sure of anything** this summer. One moment she was happy, and the next, for no reason, she was miserable. An hour ago she had loved her sneakers; now she **detested** them.

"Charlie, I'll tell you what this awful summer's been like. You remember when that finky Jim Wilson got you on the seesaw, remember that? And he kept bouncing you up and down and then he'd keep you up in the air for a real long time and then he'd drop you down real sudden, and you couldn't get off and you thought you never

....

kaleidoscope toy made of changing shapes and colors

it was a hundred everything was different

She could never be really sure of anything She did not
know what would happen next

detested hated

would? Up and down, up and down, for the rest of your life? Well, that's what this summer's been like for me."

He held out the candy and the stick to her.

"Not again!" She took it from him. "This piece of candy is so **gross** that I don't even want to touch it, if you want to know the truth." She put the stick back in and handed it to him. "Now if it comes off again—and **I mean this**, Charlie Godfrey—I'm throwing the candy away."

....

"Not again!" "You want me to help you again?"

gross dirty

I mean this I am serious

Charlie is worried about many things.
Sara understands Charlie and helps him build
a tent in the yard.

Chapter Two

Charlie looked at the empty **sucker** stick, reached into his mouth, took out the candy, and held them together in his hand. Sara had said she would throw the candy away if this happened again and so he closed his fist tightly and looked away from her.

Slowly he began to shuffle his feet back and forth on the step. He had done this so many times over the years that two grooves had been worn into the boards. It was **a nervous habit that showed he was concerned about something**, and Sara **recognized it at once**.

"All right, Charlie," she said wearily. "Where's your sucker?"

He began to shake his head slowly from side to side. His eyes were squeezed shut.

....

sucker lollipop

a nervous habit that showed he was concerned about something something he did when he felt worried

recognized it at once could see how he was feeling

"I'm not going to take it away from you. I'm going to fix it one more time."

He was unwilling to trust her and continued to shake his head. The movement was steady and mechanical, as if it would continue forever, and she watched him for a moment.

Then, with a sigh, she lifted his hand and **attempted to pry his fingers loose**. "Honestly, Charlie, you're holding onto this grubby piece of candy like it was a crown jewel or something. Now, let go." He opened his eyes and watched while she took the candy from him and put the stick in. The stick was now bent almost double, and she held it out to him carefully.

"There."

He took the sucker and held it without putting it into his mouth, still troubled by the unsteadiness of the bent stick. Sara looked down at her hands and began to pull at a broken fingernail. **There was something similar about them** in that moment, the same oval face, round brown eyes, brown hair hanging over the forehead, freckles on the nose. Then Charlie glanced up and **the illusion was broken**.

....

attempted to pry his fingers loose tried to open up his hand

There was something similar about them They looked the same

the illusion was broken they did not look the same anymore

Still holding his sucker, he looked across the yard and saw the tent he had made over the clothesline that morning. He had taken an old white blanket out into the yard, hung it over the low clothesline, and then got under it. He had sat there with the blanket blowing against him until Sara came out and said, "Charlie, you have to fasten the ends down, like this. It isn't a tent if it's just hanging in the wind."

He had thought there was something wrong. He waited beneath the blanket until she came back with some clothespins and hammered them into the hard earth, fastening the edges of the blanket to the ground. "Now, *that's* a tent."

The tent **had pleased him**. The warmth of the sun coming through the thin cotton blanket, the shadows of the trees moving overhead had made him drowsy and comfortable and now he wanted to be back in the tent.

Sara had started talking about the summer again, but he did not listen. He could tell from the tone of her voice that she was not really talking to him at all. He got up slowly and began to walk across the yard toward the tent.

....

had pleased him made him happy

Sara watched him as he walked, **a small figure for his ten years**, wearing faded blue jeans and a striped knit shirt that was stretched out of shape. He was holding the sucker in front of him as if it were a candle that might go out at any moment.

Sara said, "Don't drop that candy in the grass now or it's really going to be lost."

She watched while he bent, crawled into the tent, and sat down. The sun was behind the tent now and she could see his **silhouette**. Carefully he put the sucker back into his mouth.

Then Sara lay back on the hard boards of the porch and looked up at the ceiling.

----

a small figure for his ten years he was small for a ten-year-old
silhouette shadow

BEFORE YOU MOVE ON...

1. **Comparisons** How was this summer the same and different from other summers for Sara?

2. **Character** How did Sara treat Charlie? What did this show about Sara?

LOOK AHEAD Read pages 16–29 to find out how Wanda and Aunt Willie solve an argument.

Aunt Willie and Wanda have an argument. Sara does not want Wanda to talk to others about Charlie's problems, but Wanda disagrees.

Chapter Three

In the house Wanda and Aunt Willie were still arguing. Sara could hear every word even out on the porch. Aunt Willie, who had been taking care of them since the death of their mother six years ago, was saying loudly, "No, not on a motorcycle. No motorcycle!"

Sara **grimaced**. It was not only the loudness of Aunt Willie's voice that she disliked. It was everything—the way she **bossed them**, the way she never really listened, the way she never cared what she said. She had once announced loud enough for everyone in Carter's Drugstore to hear that Sara needed **a good dose of magnesia**.

"It isn't a motorcycle, it's a motor *scooter*." Wanda was speaking patiently, as if to a small child. "They're

....

grimaced frowned
bossed them told them what to do
a good dose of magnesia medicine for an upset stomach

practically like bicycles."

"No."

"All I want to do is to ride one half mile on this perfectly safe motor scooter—"

"No. **It's absolutely and positively no.** No!"

"Frank is very careful. He has never had even the tiniest accident."

No answer.

"Aunt Willie, it is perfectly safe. He takes his mother to the grocery store on it. Anyway, I am old enough to go without permission and I wish you'd realize it. I am nineteen years old."

No answer. Sara knew that Aunt Willie would be standing by the sink shaking her head emphatically from side to side.

"Aunt Willie, he's going to be here any minute. He's coming all the way over here just to drive me to the lake to see the swans."

"You don't care *that* for seeing those swans."

"I do too. I love birds."

"All right then, those swans have been on the lake three days, and not once have you gone over to see them.

....

It's absolutely and positively no. You cannot go.

You don't care *that* for You do not care about

Now all of a sudden you *have* to go, can't wait one minute
to get on this devil motorcycle and see those swans."

"For your information, **I have been dying to see them**,
only this is my first chance." She went out of the kitchen
and pulled the swinging door shut behind her. "And I'm
going," she said over her shoulder.

Wanda came out of the house, slammed the screen
door, stepped over Boysie, and sat by Sara on the top step.
"She never wants anyone to have any fun."

"I know."

"She makes me so mad. All I want to do is just ride
down to see the swans on Frank's motor scooter." She
looked at Sara, then **broke off** and said, "Where did
Charlie go?"

"He's over there in his tent."

"I see him now. I wish Frank would hurry up and get
here before Aunt Willie comes out." She stood, looked
down the street, and sat back on the steps. "Did I tell you
what that boy in my psychology class last year said about
Charlie?"

Sara straightened. "What boy?"

"This boy Arnold Hampton, in my psychology class.

....

I have been dying to see them I want to see them very much
broke off stopped

18

We were discussing children who—"

"You mean you talk about Charlie to **perfect strangers**? To your class? I think that's awful." She put her feet into the two grooves worn in the steps by Charlie. "What do you say? 'Let me tell you all about **my retarded brother**—it's so interesting'?" It was the first time in her life that she had used the term "retarded" in connection with her brother, and she looked quickly away from the figure in the white tent. Her face felt suddenly hot and she snapped a leaf from the rhododendron bush by the steps and held it against her forehead.

"No, I don't say that. Honestly, Sara, you—"

"And then do you say, 'And while I'm telling you about my retarded brother, I'll also tell you about my **real hung-up sister**'?" She moved the leaf to her lips and blew against it angrily.

"No, I don't say that because you're not all that fascinating, if you want to know the truth. Anyway, Arnold Hampton's father happens to be a **pediatrician** and Arnold is sincerely interested in working with boys like Charlie. He is even helping start a camp which Charlie

....

perfect strangers people you don't even know
my retarded brother my brother who has a mental disability
real hung-up sister sister and all her problems
pediatrician children's doctor

may get to go to next summer, and all because I talked to him in my psychology class." She sighed. "**You're impossible**, you know that? I can't imagine why I even try to tell you anything."

"Well, Charlie's our problem."

"He's everybody's. There is no—Oh, here comes Frank." She broke off and got to her feet. "Tell Aunt Willie I'll be home later."

She started quickly down the walk, waving to the boy who was making his way slowly up the street on a green motor scooter.

You're impossible I cannot talk to you

Frank takes Aunt Willie for a ride on his motor scooter. Sara does not want to take Charlie to the lake to see the swans.

Chapter Four

"Wait, wait, you wait." Aunt Willie came onto the porch drying her hands on a dish towel. She stood at the top of the steps until Frank, a thin boy with red hair, brought the motor scooter to a stop. As he **kicked down the stand** she called out, "Frank, listen, save yourself some steps. Wanda's not going anywhere on that motorcycle."

"Aw, Aunt Willie," Frank said. He opened the gate and came slowly up the walk. "All we're going to do is go down to the lake. We don't even have to get on the highway for that."

"No motorcycles," she said. "You go break your neck if you want to. **That's not my business.** Wanda, **left in my care**, is not going to break her neck on any motorcycle."

"Nobody's going to break his neck. We're just going to have a very uneventful ride down the road to the

....

kicked down the stand parked the scooter
That's not my business. I cannot stop you.
left in my care who I am taking care of

lake. Then we're going to turn around and have a very uneventful ride back."

"No."

"I tell you what," Frank said. **"I'll make a deal with you."**

"What deal?"

"Have you ever been on a motor scooter?"

"Me? I never even rode on a bicycle."

"Try it. Come on. I'll ride you down to the Tennents' house and back. Then if you think it's not safe, you say to me, 'Frank, it's not safe,' and I'll take my motor scooter and ride off into the sunset."

She hesitated. There was something about a ride that **appealed to her.**

Sara said against the rhododendron leaf, "I don't think you **ought to**. You're too old to be riding up and down the street on a motor scooter."

She knew instantly she had said the wrong thing, for at once Aunt Willie turned to her angrily. "Too old!" She faced Sara with indignation. "I am barely forty years old. May I grow a beard if I'm not." She stepped closer, her voice rising. "Who says I'm so old?" She held the dish

....

"I'll make a deal with you." "I have a plan that we will both like."

appealed to her she liked; interested her

ought to should take a ride

towel in front of her, like a matador taunting a bull. The dish towel flicked the air once.

"Nobody said anything," Sara said wearily. She threw the leaf down and brushed it off the steps with her foot.

"Then where did all this talk about my age come from, I'd like to know?"

"Anyway," Frank interrupted, "you're not too old to ride a motor scooter."

"I'll do it." She threw the dish towel across the chair and went down the steps. "I may break my neck but I'll do it."

"Hold on tight, Aunt Willie," Wanda called.

"Hold on! Listen, my hands never held on to anything the way I'm going to hold on to this motorcycle." She laughed, then said to Frank, "I never rode on one of these before, believe me."

"It's just like a motorized baby carriage, Aunt Willie."
"Huh!"

"This ought to be good," Wanda said. She called, "Hey, Charlie," waited until he looked out from the tent, and then said, "Watch Aunt Willie. She's going to ride the motor scooter."

....

It's just like a motorized baby carriage It is safe enough for a baby to ride

This ought to be good This will be fun to watch

Charlie watched Aunt Willie **settle herself sidesaddle** on the back of the scooter.

"Ready?" Frank asked.

"I'm as ready as I'll ever be, believe me, go on, go on."

Her words rose into a piercing scream as Frank moved the scooter forward, turned, and then started down the hill. Her scream, shrill as a bird's cry, hung in the still air. "Frank, Frank, Frank, Frankeeeeee!"

At the first cry Charlie staggered to his feet, staring **in alarm** at Aunt Willie disappearing down the hill. He pulled on one side of the tent as he got to his feet, causing the other to snap loose at the ground and hang limp from the line. He stumbled, then regained his balance.

Wanda saw him and said, "It's all right, Charlie, she's having a good time. She *likes* it. It's all right." She crossed the yard, took him by the hand, and led him to the steps. "What have you got all over yourself?"

"It's a gross red sucker," Sara said. "It's all over me, too."

"Come on over to the **spigot** and let me wash your hands. See, Aunt Willie's coming back now."

....

settle herself sidesaddle sit sideways

in alarm in a worried way

spigot water faucet

In front of the Tennents' house Frank was swinging the scooter around, pivoting on one foot, and Aunt Willie stopped screaming long enough to call to the Tennents, "Bernie, Midge, look who's on a motorcycle!" Then she began screaming again as Frank started the uphill climb. As they came to a stop Aunt Willie's cries changed to laughter. "Huh, old woman, am I! Old woman!" Still laughing, she stepped off the scooter.

"You're all right, Aunt Willie," Frank said.

Sensing a moment of advantage, Wanda moved down the walk. She was shaking the water from her hands. "So can I go, Aunt Willie?"

"Oh, go on, go on," she said, half laughing, half scolding. "**It's your own neck.** Go on, break your own neck if you want to."

"It's not her neck you have to worry about, it's my arms," Frank said. "Honest, Aunt Willie, **there's not a drop of blood circulating in them**."

"Oh, go on, go on with you."

"Come on, Little One," Frank said to Wanda.

Aunt Willie came and stood by Sara, and they watched

....

Sensing a moment of advantage Seeing that Aunt Willie was happy

It's your own neck. It will be your fault if you get hurt.

there's not a drop of blood circulating in them my arms are numb

Wanda climb on the back of the motor scooter. As Wanda and Frank drove off, Aunt Willie laughed again and said, "Next thing, *you'll* be going off with some boy on a motorcycle."

Sara had been smiling, but at once she stopped and looked down at her hands. "I don't think you have to worry about that."

"Huh! It will happen, you'll see. You'll be just like Wanda. You'll be—"

"Don't you see that I'm nothing like Wanda at all?" She sat down abruptly and put her lips against her knees. "We are so different. Wanda is a hundred times prettier than I am."

"You are just alike, you two. Sometimes in the kitchen I hear you and I think I'm hearing Wanda. That's how alike you are. **May my ears fall off if I can** hear the difference."

"Maybe our *voices* are alike, but that's all. I can make my voice sound like a hundred different people. Listen to this and guess who it is. 'N-B-C! Beautiful downtown Burbank.'"

"**I'm not in the mood for** a guessing game. I'm in the

....

May my ears fall off if I can I really can never
I'm not in the mood for I do not want to play

mood to get back to our original conversation. **It's not how you look that's important**, let me tell you. I had a sister so beautiful you wouldn't believe it."

"Who?"

"Frances, that's who."

"She wasn't all that beautiful. I've seen her and—"

"When she was young she was. So beautiful you wouldn't believe it, but such a devil, and—"

"It is *too* important how you look. Parents are always saying it's not how you look that counts. I've heard that all my life. It doesn't matter how you look. It doesn't matter how you look. Huh! If you want to find out how much it matters, just let your hair get too long or put on too much eye makeup and listen to the screams." She got up abruptly and said, "I think I'll walk over and see the swans myself."

"Well, I **have not finished with this conversation yet**, young lady."

Sara turned and looked at Aunt Willie, waited with her hands jammed into her back pockets.

"Oh, never mind," Aunt Willie said, picking up her dish towel and shaking it. "I might as well hold a

....

It's not how you look that's important It does not matter what you look like

have not finished with this conversation yet am not done talking to you about this

conversation with this towel as with you when you get that look on your face. Go on and see the swans." She broke off. "Hey, Charlie, you want to go with Sara to see the swans?"

"He'll get too tired," Sara said.

"So walk slow."

"I never get to do anything **by myself**. I have to take him everywhere. I have him all day and Wanda all night. In all this whole house I have one drawer **to myself**. *One drawer.*"

"Get up, Charlie. Sara's going to take you to see the swans."

Sara looked down into his eyes and said, "Oh, come on," and **drew him to his feet**.

"Wait, there's some bread from supper." Aunt Willie ran into the house and came back with four rolls. "Take them. Here. Let Charlie feed the swans."

"Well, come on, Charlie, or it's going to be dark before we get there."

"Don't you rush him along, hear me, Sara?"

"I won't."

....

by myself alone

to myself that is mine

drew him to his feet helped him stand up

Holding Sara's hand, Charlie went slowly down the walk. He hesitated at the gate and then moved with her onto the sidewalk. As they walked down the hill, his feet made a continuous scratching sound on the concrete.

BEFORE YOU MOVE ON...

1. **Character** Why did Aunt Willie let Wanda ride the scooter? What does this show about Aunt Willie?

2. **Character's Point of View** Reread page 28. Why didn't Sara want to bring Charlie to the lake? What made her change her mind?

LOOK AHEAD Read pages 30–38 to find out what is important about Charlie's watch.

On the way to the lake, Sara stops at her friend Mary's house. Charlie waits outside while the two friends talk.

Chapter Five

When they were **out of earshot** Sara said, "Aunt Willie thinks she knows everything. I get so sick of hearing how I am exactly like Wanda when Wanda is beautiful. I think she's just beautiful. If I could look like anyone in the world, I would want to look like her." She kicked at some high grass by the sidewalk. "And it does too matter how you look, I can tell you that." She walked ahead angrily for a few steps, then waited for Charlie and took his hand again.

"I think how you look is the most important thing in the world. If you *look* cute, you *are* cute; if you *look* smart, you *are* smart, and if you don't look like anything, then you aren't anything.

"I wrote **a theme** on that one time in school, about

---

out of earshot too far away for Aunt Willie to hear

a theme a paper for school; an essay

looks being the most important thing in the world, and I got a D—a *D*! Which is a terrible grade.

"After class the teacher called me up and told me **the same old business** about looks not being important, and how some of the ugliest people in the world were the smartest and kindest and cleverest."

They walked past the Tennents' house just as someone inside turned on the television, and they heard Eddie Albert singing, "Greeeeeeen acres is—" before it was turned down. Charlie paused a moment, recognizing the beginning of one of his favorite programs, looked up at Sara, and waited.

"Come on," Sara said. "And then there was this girl in my English class named Thelma Louise and she wrote a paper entitled 'Making People Happy' and she got an A. An *A*! Which is as good as you can get. It was sickening. Thelma Louise is a beautiful girl with blond hair and naturally curly eyelashes, so **what does she know**? Anyway, one time Hazel went over to Thelma Louise's, and she said the rug was worn thin in front of the mirror in Thelma Louise's room because Thelma Louise stood there all the time watching herself."

....

the same old business the same thing Aunt Willie said
what does she know how could she understand

She sighed and continued to walk. Most of the houses were set close together as if huddled for safety, and on either side of the houses the West Virginia hills rose, black now in the early evening shadows. The hills were as they had been for hundreds of years, rugged forest land, except that **strip mining had begun** on the hills to the north, and the trees and earth had been **hacked away**, leaving unnatural cliffs of pale washed earth.

Sara paused. They were now in front of Mary Weicek's house and she said, "Stop a minute. I've got to speak to Mary." She could hear Mary's record player, and she **longed to be up** in Mary's room, leaning back against the pink dotted bedspread listening to Mary's endless collection of records. "Mary!" she called. "You want to walk to the pond with me and Charlie and see the swans?"

Mary came to the window. "Wait, I'm coming out."

Sara waited on the sidewalk until Mary came out into the yard. "I can't go because my cousin's here and she's going to cut my hair," Mary said, "but did you get your dress yesterday?"

"No."

---

strip mining had begun people had started digging up the land
hacked away cut
longed to be up wished she could be

"Why not? I thought your aunt said you could."

"She did, but when we got in the store and she saw how much it cost she said it was foolish to pay so much for a dress when she could make me one just like it."

"Disappointment."

"Yes, because unfortunately she can't make one *just* like it, she can only make one **kind of like it**. You remember how the stripes **came together diagonally** in the front of that dress? Well, she already has mine cut out and I can see that not one stripe meets."

"Oh, Sara."

"I could see when she was cutting it that the stripes weren't going to meet and I kept saying, 'It's not right, Aunt Willie, the stripes aren't going to meet,' and all the while I'm screaming, the scissors are flashing and she is muttering, 'The stripes will meet, the stripes will meet,' and then she holds it up **in great triumph** and not one stripe meets."

"That's awful, because I remember thinking when you showed me the dress that it was the way the stripes met that looked so good."

....

kind of like it that looks a little like the other dress
came together diagonally met each other
in great triumph thinking she has done a good job,

"**I am aware of that.** It now makes me look like one half of my body is about two inches lower than the other half."

"Listen, come on in and watch my cousin cut my hair, can you?"

"I better not. I promised Aunt Willie I'd take Charlie to see the swans."

"Well, just come in and see how she's going to cut it. She has a whole book of hair styles."

"Oh, all right, for a minute. Charlie, you sit down right there." She pointed to the steps. "Right there now and don't move, hear me? Don't move off that step. Don't even stand up." Then she went in the house with Mary, saying, "I really **can't stay but** a minute because I've got to take Charlie down to see the swans and then I've got to get home in time to dye my **tennis shoes**—"

"Which ones?"

"These, these awful orange things. They make me look like Donald Duck or something."

....

I am aware of that. I know that.
can't stay but can only stay for
tennis shoes sneakers

As Charlie waits for Sara, he plays with his watch. Mary's mother and friend talk about what happened to Charlie when he was young. Then Charlie and Sara leave for the lake.

Chapter Six

Charlie sat in the sudden stillness, hunched over his knees, on the bottom step. The whole world seemed to have been turned off when Sara went into the Weiceks' house, and he did not move for a long time. The only sound was the ticking of his watch.

The watch **was a great pleasure to him**. He **had no knowledge of** hours or minutes, but he liked to listen to it and to watch the small red hand moving around the dial, counting off the seconds, and it was he who remembered every morning after breakfast to have Aunt Willie **wind it for him**. Now he rested his arm across his legs and looked at the watch.

....

was a great pleasure to him made him very happy
had no knowledge of did not understand
wind it for him turn the watch stem so that it would keep working

He had a lonely feeling. He got this whenever he was by himself in a strange place, and he turned quickly when he heard the screen door open to see if it was Sara. When he saw Mrs. Weicek and another woman he turned back and looked at his watch. As he bent over, a pale half circle of flesh showed between the back of his shirt and his pants.

"Who's the little boy, Allie?"

Mrs. Weicek said, "That's Sara's brother, Charlie. You remember me telling you about him. He's the one that can't talk. Hasn't spoken a word since he was three years old."

"Doesn't talk at all?"

"If he does, no one's ever heard him, not since his illness. He can understand what you say to him, and he goes to school, and they say he can write the alphabet, but he can't talk."

Charlie did not hear them. He put his ear against his watch and listened to the sound. There was something about the rhythmic ticking that **never failed to soothe him**. The watch was **a magic charm** whose tiny noise and movements could **block out the whole clamoring world**.

....

never failed to soothe him always made him feel better

a magic charm something special

block out the whole clamoring world quiet down all of the noises around him

Mrs. Weicek said, "Ask him what time it is, Ernestine. He is so proud of that watch. Everyone always asks him what time it is." Then without waiting, she herself said, "What time is it, Charlie? What time is it?"

He turned and obediently held out the arm with the watch on it.

"My goodness, it's after eight o'clock," Mrs. Weicek said. "Thank you, Charlie. Charlie keeps everyone informed of the time. **We just couldn't get along without him.**"

The two women sat in the rocking chairs on the porch, moving slowly back and forth. The noise of the chairs and the creaking floor boards made Charlie forget the watch for a moment. He got slowly to his feet and stood looking up the street.

"Sit down, Charlie, and wait for Sara," Mrs. Weicek said.

Without looking at her, he began to walk toward the street.

"Charlie, Sara wants you to wait for her."

"Maybe he doesn't hear you, Allie."

"He hears me all right. Charlie, wait for Sara. Wait now." Then she called, "Sara, your brother's leaving."

....

We just couldn't get along without him. We need him to tell us the time.

Sara looked out the upstairs window and said, "All right, Charlie, I'm coming. Will you wait for a minute? Mary, I've got to go."

She ran out of the house and caught Charlie by the arm. "What are you going home for? Don't you want to see the swans?"

He stood without looking at her.

"Honestly, I leave you alone for one second and **off you go**. Now come on." She tugged his arm impatiently.

As they started down the hill together she waved to Mary, who was at the window, and said to Charlie, "I hope the swans are worth all this trouble I'm going to."

"We'll probably get there and they'll be gone," she added. They walked in silence. Then Sara said, "Here's where we cut across the field." She waited while he stepped carefully over the narrow ditch, and then the two of them walked across the field **side by side**, Sara kicking her feet restlessly in the deep grass.

....

off you go you get up and leave

side by side next to each other

BEFORE YOU MOVE ON...

1. **Metaphor** To Charlie, the watch is a "magic charm." Tell what this means in your own words.

2. **Character's Motive** Reread page 37. Why did Mrs. Weicek ask Charlie what time it was?

LOOK AHEAD Read pages 39–45 to find out why this summer is different for Sara.

Charlie and Sara watch the swans at the lake.
Soon, Sara is ready to go, but Charlie does
not want to leave yet.

Chapter Seven

There was something painfully beautiful about the swans. The whiteness, the elegance of them on this dark lake, the incredible ease of their movements **made Sara catch her breath** as she and Charlie **rounded the dump of pines**.

"There they are, Charlie."

She could tell the exact moment he saw them because his hand tightened; he really held her hand for the first time since they had left Mary's. Then he stopped.

"There are the swans."

The six swans seemed motionless on the water, their necks all arched at the same angle, so that it seemed there was only one swan mirrored five times.

"There are the swans," she said again. She felt she

....

made Sara catch her breath surprised Sara
rounded the dump of pines walked past the pine trees

would like to stand there **pointing out the swans** to
Charlie for the rest of the summer. She watched as they
drifted slowly across the water.

"Hey, Sara!"

She looked across the lake and saw Wanda and Frank,
who had come by the road. "Sara, listen, tell Aunt Willie
that Frank and I are going over to his sister's to see her
new baby."

"All right."

"I'll be home at eleven."

She watched as Wanda and Frank got back on the
motor scooter. **At the roar of the scooter**, the startled
swans changed direction and moved toward Sara. She and
Charlie walked closer to the lake.

"The swans are coming over here, Charlie. They see
you, I believe."

They watched in silence for a moment as the sound
of the scooter faded. Then Sara sat down on the grass,
crossed her legs **yoga style**, and picked out a stick which
was **wedged** inside one of the orange tennis shoes.

"Sit down, Charlie. Don't just stand there."

....

pointing out the swans showing the swans
At the roar of the scooter When the scooter started up
yoga style in front of her body
wedged stuck

Awkwardly, with his legs angled out in front of him, he sat on the grass. Sara pulled off a piece of a roll and tossed it to the swans. "Now they'll come over here," she said. "They love bread."

She paused, put a piece of roll into her own mouth, and sat chewing for a moment.

"I saw the swans when they flew here, did you know that, Charlie? I was out on our porch last Friday and I looked up, and they were coming over the house and they looked so funny, like frying pans with their necks stretched out." She handed him a roll. "Here. Give the swans something to eat. Look, watch me. **Like that.**"

She watched him, then said, "No, Charlie, small pieces, because swans get things caught in their throats easily. No, that's *too* little. That's just a crumb. Like *that*."

She watched while he threw the bread into the pond, then said, "You know where the swans live **most of the time**? At the university, which is a big school, and right in the middle of this university is a lake and that's where the swans live. Only sometimes, for no reason, the swans decide to fly away, and off they go to another pond or

....

Like that. Do what I just did.

most of the time when they are not here

another lake. This one isn't half as pretty as the lake at the university, but here they are."

She handed Charlie another roll. "Anyway, that's what Wanda thinks, because the swans at the university are gone."

Charlie turned, **motioned that** he wanted another roll for the swans, and she gave him the last one. He threw it into the water in four large pieces and put out his hand for another.

"No more. That's all." She showed him her empty hands.

One of the swans dived under the water and rose to shake its feathers. Then it moved across the water. Slowly the other swans followed, dipping their long necks far into the water to catch any remaining pieces of bread.

Sara leaned forward and put her hands on Charlie's shoulders. His body felt soft, as if the muscles had never been used. "The swans are exactly alike," she said. "Exactly. **No one can tell them apart.**"

She began to rub Charlie's back slowly, carefully. Then she stopped abruptly and clapped him on the shoulders. "Well, let's go home."

....

motioned that moved his hands to show that

No one can tell them apart. They look the same to everyone.

He sat without moving, still looking at the swans on the other side of the lake.

"Come on, Charlie." She knew he had heard her, yet he still did not move. "Come *on*." She **got to her feet and stood looking** down at him. She held out her hand to help him up, but he did not even glance at her. He continued to watch the swans.

"Come on, Charlie. Mary may come up later and help me dye my shoes." She looked at him, then snatched a leaf from the **limb** overhead and threw it at the water. She waited, stuck her hands in her back pockets, and said tiredly, "Come on, Charlie."

He began to shake his head slowly back and forth without looking at her.

"Mary's coming up to help me dye my shoes and if you don't come on we won't have time to do them and I'll end up wearing these same awful Donald Duck shoes all year. Come *on*."

He continued to shake his head back and forth.

"This is why I never want to bring you anywhere, because you won't go home when I'm ready."

With his fingers he began to hold the long grass on

....

got to her feet and stood looking stood up and looked
limb tree branch

either side of him as if this would help him if she tried to pull him to his feet.

"**You are really irritating**, you know that?" He did not look at her and she sighed and said, "All right, if I stay five more minutes, will you go?" She bent down and showed him on his watch. "That's to right there. When the big hand gets *there*, we go home, all right?"

He nodded.

"**Promise?**"

He nodded again.

"All right." There was a tree that hung over the water and she went and leaned against it. "All right, Charlie, four more minutes now," she called.

Already he had started shaking his head again, all the while watching the swans gliding across the dark water.

Squinting up at the sky, Sara began to kick her foot back and forth in the deep grass. "In just a month, Charlie, the summer will be over," she said without looking at him, "and I will be so glad."

Up until this year, it seemed, her life had **flowed along with rhythmic evenness**. The first fourteen years of her life all seemed the same. She had loved her sister without

....

You are really irritating You make me angry

"Promise?" "Will you do what I said?"

flowed along with rhythmic evenness been the same every day

44

envy, her aunt without finding her coarse, her brother without pity. Now all that was changed. She **was filled with a discontent**, an anger about herself, her life, her family, that made her think she would **never be content** again.

She turned and looked at the swans. The sudden, unexpected tears in her eyes blurred the images of the swans into white circles, and she blinked. Then she said aloud, "Three minutes, Charlie."

....

was filled with a discontent had a strange feeling inside
never be content never feel happy and safe

BEFORE YOU MOVE ON...

1. **Comparisons** Reread pages 44–45. The first fourteen years of Sara's life all seemed the same. What was different this summer?

2. **Conclusions** How did Charlie and Sara feel when they watched the swans?

LOOK AHEAD Read pages 46–54 to find out why Sara feels so unhappy.

That night, Sara tries to explain her feelings to Wanda. Then Sara cannot sleep because she hears Charlie in the room next door.

Chapter Eight

Sara was lying in bed with the lights out when Wanda came into the bedroom that night. Sara was wearing an old pair of her father's pajamas with the sleeves cut out and the legs rolled up. She watched as Wanda moved quietly across the room and then stumbled over the dressing-table stool. **Hobbling** on one foot, Wanda opened the closet door and turned on the light.

"You can put on the big light if you want. I'm awake," Sara said.

"*Now* you tell me."

"Did you have a good time, Wanda?"

"Yes."

"Did you get to see the baby?"

"He was so cute. He looked exactly like Frank. You wouldn't have believed it."

....

Hobbling Moving painfully; Stumbling

"*Now* you tell me." "You should have told me before I got hurt."

"Poor baby."

"No, he was darling, really he was, with little red curls all over his head." She undressed quickly, turned off the closet light, and then got into bed beside Sara. She smoothed her pillow and looked up at the ceiling. "Frank is so nice, don't you think?"

"He's all right."

"Don't you like him?" She rose up on one elbow and looked down at Sara in the big striped pajamas.

"I said he was all right."

"Well, what don't you like?"

"I didn't say I didn't like him."

"I know, but **I can tell**. What don't you like?"

"For one thing, **he never pays any attention to** Charlie. When he came up the walk tonight he didn't even speak to him."

"He probably didn't see him in the tent. Anyway, he likes Charlie—he told me so. What else?"

"Oh, nothing, it's just that he's always so **affected**, the way he calls you Little One and gives you those real meaningful movie-star looks."

"I love it when he calls me Little One. Just wait till

....

I can tell I know how you feel

he never pays any attention to he doesn't care about

affected fake

someone calls *you* Little One."

"I'd like to know who could call me Little One except the Jolly Green Giant."

"Oh, Sara."

"Well, I'm bigger than everyone I know."

"You'll find someone."

"Yes, maybe if I'm lucky I'll meet somebody from some weird foreign country where men value tall skinny girls with big feet and crooked noses. Every time I see a movie, though, even if it takes place in the weirdest, foreignest country in the world, like where women dance in gauze bloomers and tin bras, the women are still little and beautiful." Then she said, "Anyway, I hate boys. **They're all just one big nothing.**"

"Sara, what's wrong with you?"

"Nothing."

"No, I mean it. What's really wrong?"

"I don't know. I just feel awful."

"Physically awful?"

"Now **don't start being the nurse**."

"Well, I want to know."

They're all just one big nothing. They are not important to me.

"Physically awful?" "Are you sick?"

don't start being the nurse don't act like a nurse

"No, **not physically awful, just plain awful**. I feel like I want to start screaming and kicking and I want to jump up and tear down the curtains and rip up the sheets and hammer holes in the walls. I want to yank my clothes out of the closet and burn them and—"

"Well, why don't you try it if it would make you feel better?"

"Because it wouldn't." She lifted the top sheet and watched as it billowed in the air and then lowered on her body. She could feel the cloth as it settled on the bare part of her legs. "I just feel like nothing."

"Oh, everybody does at times, Sara."

"Not like me. I'm not anything. I'm not cute, and I'm not pretty, and I'm not a good dancer, and I'm not smart, and **I'm not popular**. I'm not anything."

"You're a good dishwasher."

"Shut up, Wanda. I don't think that's funny."

"Welllll—"

"You act like you want to talk to me and then you start being funny. You do that to me all the time."

"I'm through being funny, so go on."

"Well, if you could see some of the girls in my school you'd know what I mean. They look like models. Their

....

not physically awful, just plain awful I don't feel sick, just sad
I'm not popular I don't have a lot of friends

49

clothes are so **tuff** and they're invited to every party, every dance, by about ten boys and when they walk down the hall everybody turns and looks at them."

"Oh, those girls. **They hit the peak of their whole lives** in junior high school. They look like grown women in eighth grade with the big teased hair and the eye liner and by the time they're in high school they **have a used look**."

"Well, I certainly don't have to worry about getting a used look."

"I think it is really sad to hit the peak of your whole life in junior high school."

"Girls, quit that arguing," Aunt Willie called from her room. "I can hear you all the way in here."

"We're not arguing," Wanda called back. "We are having a peaceful little discussion."

"I know an argument when I hear one, believe me. That's one thing I've heard plenty of and I'm hearing one right now. Be quiet and go to sleep."

"All right."

They lay in silence. Sara said, "The peak of my whole life so far was in third grade when I got to be milk monitor."

....

tuff cute, trendy

They hit the peak of their whole lives The best time of their lives is

have a used look they look old and tired

Wanda laughed. **"Just give yourself a little time."** She reached over, turned on the radio, and waited till it warmed up. "Frank's going to **dedicate a song to me on the Diamond Jim show**," she said. "Will the radio bother you?"

"No."

"Well, it bothers me," Aunt Willie called from her room. "Maybe you two can sleep with the radio blaring and people arguing, but I can't."

"I have just barely got the radio turned on, Aunt Willie. I have to put my head practically on the table to even hear it." She broke off abruptly. "What was that dedication, did you hear?"

"It was to all the girls on the second floor of Arnold Hall."

"Oh."

"I mean what I say now," Aunt Willie called. "You two get to sleep. Wanda, you've got to be up early to get to your job at the hospital on time, even if Sara can spend the whole day in bed."

"I'd like to know how I can spend the whole day in bed when she gets me up at eight o'clock," Sara grumbled.

....

"Just give yourself a little time." "Things will get better soon."
dedicate a song to me on the Diamond Jim show ask the radio station to play a song for me

51

"Aunt Willie, I just want to hear my dedication and then I'll go to sleep."

Silence.

Sara turned over on her side with the sheet wrapped tightly around her body and closed her eyes. She was not sleepy now. She could hear the music from the radio, and the sound from the next room of Charlie turning over in his bed, trying to get settled, then turning over again. She pulled the pillow over her head, but she could not block out the noises. Oddly, it was the restless sounds from Charlie's room which seemed loudest.

Charlie **was not a good sleeper**. When he was three, he had had two illnesses, one following the other, terrible high-fevered illnesses, which had almost **taken his life** and had damaged his brain. Afterward, he had lain silent and still in his bed, and it had been strange to Sara to see **the pale baby that had replaced the hot, flushed, tormented one.** The once-bright eyes were slow to follow what was before them, and the hands never reached out, even when Sara held her brother's favorite stuffed dog, Buh-Buh, above him. He rarely cried, never laughed. Now it was as if Charlie wanted to make up for those listless years in bed

....

was not a good sleeper did not sleep well

taken his life killed him

the pale baby that had replaced the hot, flushed, tormented one that her sick brother was now pale and quiet

by never sleeping again.

Sara heard his foot thump against the wall. It was a thing that could continue for hours, a faint sound that no one seemed to hear but Sara, who slept against the wall. With a sigh she put the pillow back beneath her head and looked up at the ceiling.

"That was my dedication. Did you hear it?" Wanda whispered. "To Little One from Frank."

"Vomit."

"Well, **I think it was sweet**."

The thumping against the wall stopped, then began again. It was a sound that Sara had become used to, but tonight it seemed unusually loud. She found herself thinking how this had been Charlie's first movement after his long illness, a restless kicking out of one foot, a weak movement then that could hardly be noticed beneath the covers, but now, tonight, one that seemed to make the whole house tremble.

"Don't tell me you don't hear that," she said to Wanda. "I don't see how you can all **persist in saying** that you don't hear Charlie kicking the wall."

Silence.

···

"Vomit." "That makes me feel sick."

I think it was sweet I liked it

persist in saying keep saying

"Wanda, are you asleep?"

Silence.

"Honestly, I don't see how people can just fall asleep any time they want to. Wanda, are you really asleep?"

She waited, then **drew the sheet close about** her neck and turned to the wall.

....

drew the sheet close about pulled the bed sheet up to

BEFORE YOU MOVE ON...

1. **Character's Point of View** Reread page 49. What did Sara mean when she said, "I just feel like nothing"?

2. **Cause and Effect** Reread page 52. What had happened to Charlie because of his illnesses?

LOOK AHEAD Read pages 55–65 to find out what Charlie decides to do.

Charlie is worried and unhappy, but no one helps him. Late that night, he gets up and goes to look for the swans.

Chapter Nine

In his room Charlie lay in bed still kicking his foot against the wall. He was not asleep but was staring up at the ceiling where the shadows were moving. He never went to sleep easily, but tonight he had been **concerned** because a button was missing from his pajamas, and **sleep was impossible.** He had shown the place where the button was missing to Aunt Willie when he was ready for bed, but she had patted his shoulder and said, "I'll fix it tomorrow," and gone back to watching a game show on television.

"Look at that," Aunt Willie was saying to herself. "They're never going to guess the name. How can famous celebrities be so stupid?" She had leaned forward and shouted at the **panelists,** "It's Clark Gable!" Then, "Have they never heard of a person who works in a store? A

....

concerned very worried
sleep was impossible he would never be able to fall asleep
panelists people on the game show

person who works in a store is a *clerk*—Clerk Gable—the name is *Clerk Gable*!"

Charlie had touched her on the shoulder and tried again to show her the pajamas.

"I'll fix it tomorrow, Charlie." She had **waved him away with one hand**.

He had gone back into the kitchen, where Sara was dyeing her tennis shoes in the sink.

"Don't show it to me," she said. "I can't look at anything right now. And Mary, quit laughing at my tennis shoes."

"I can't help it. They're so gross."

Sara lifted them out of the sink with two spoons. "I know they're gross, only you should have told me that orange tennis shoes could not be dyed baby blue. Look at that. That is the worst color you have ever seen in your life. Admit it."

"I admit it."

"Well, you don't have to admit it so quickly. They **ought to put** on the dye wrapper that orange cannot be dyed baby blue. A warning."

"They do."

....

waved him away with one hand waved a hand to tell him to go away

ought to put should write

"Well, they ought to put it in big letters. Look at those shoes. There must be a terrible name for that color."

"There is," Mary said. "Puce."

"What?"

"Puce."

"Mary Weicek, you made that up."

"I did not. It really is a color."

"I have never heard a word that describes anything better. Puce. These just look like puce shoes, don't they?" She set them on newspapers. "They're—Charlie, get out of the way, please, or I'm going to get dye all over you."

He stepped back, still holding his pajama jacket out in front of him. There were times when he could not get anyone's attention no matter what he did. He took Sara's arm and she **shrugged free**.

"Charlie, there's not a button on anything I own, either, so go on to bed."

Slowly, **filled with dissatisfaction**, he had gone to his room and got into bed. There he had begun to pull worriedly at the empty buttonhole until the cloth had started to tear, and then he had continued to pull until the whole front of his pajama top was torn and hung open.

....

shrugged free moved around until he let go
filled with dissatisfaction feeling sad and unhappy

He was now holding the jacket partly closed with his hands and looking up at the ceiling.

It was one o'clock and Charlie had been lying there for three hours.

He heard a noise outside, and for the first time he forgot about his pajamas. He stopped kicking his foot against the wall, sat up, and looked out the window. There was something white in the bushes; he could see it moving.

He released his pajamas and held onto the window sill tightly, because he thought that he had just seen one of the swans outside his window, gliding slowly through the leaves. The memory of their soft smoothness in the water came to him and **warmed him**.

He got out of bed and stood by the other window. He heard a cat miaowing and saw the Hutchinsons' white cat from next door, but he paid no attention to it. **The swans were fixed with such certainty in his mind** that he could not even imagine that what he had seen was only the cat.

Still looking for the swans, he pressed his face against the screen. The beauty of them, the whiteness, the softness, the silent splendor had impressed him greatly,

....

warmed him made him feel better
The swans were fixed with such certainty in his mind He was so sure that he had seen the swans

and he **felt a longing to be once again by the lake**, sitting in the deep grass, throwing bread to the waiting swans.

It occurred to him suddenly that the swan outside the window had come to find him, and with a small pleased smile he went around the bed, sat, and slowly began to put on his bedroom slippers. Then he walked out into the hall. His feet made a quiet shuffling sound as he passed through the linoleumed hall and into the living room, but no one heard him.

The front door had been left open **for coolness** and only the screen door was latched. Charlie lifted the hook, pushed open the door, and stepped out onto the porch. Boysie, who slept in the kitchen, heard the door shut and came to the living room. He whined softly when he saw Charlie outside on the porch and scratched at the door. He waited, then after a moment went back to the kitchen and curled up on his rug in front of the sink.

Charlie walked across the front porch and sat on the steps. He waited. He was patient at first, for he thought that the swans would come to the steps, but as time passed and they did not come, he began to shuffle his feet impatiently back and forth on the third step.

....

felt a longing to be once again by the lake wanted to go to be by the lake again

for coolness to keep the house cool

Suddenly he saw something white in the bushes. He got up and, holding the **banister**, went down the steps and crossed the yard. He looked into the bushes, but the swans were not there. It was only the cat, crouched down behind the leaves and looking up at him with slitted eyes.

He stood there, looking at the cat, unable to understand what had happened to the swans. He rubbed his hands up and down his pajama tops, pulling at the torn material. The cat darted further back into the bushes and disappeared.

After a moment Charlie turned and began to walk slowly across the yard. He went to the gate and paused. He had been told again and again that he must never go out of the yard, but those instructions, given in daylight with noisy traffic on the street, **seemed to have nothing to do with the present situation**.

In the soft darkness all the things that usually confused him—speeding bicycles, loud noises, lawn mowers, barking dogs, shouting children—were gone, replaced by silence and a silvery moonlit darkness. He seemed to belong to this silent world far more than he belonged to the daytime world of **feverish activity**.

....

banister railing on the stairs

seemed to have nothing to do with the present situation
did not seem important now

feverish activity noise and movement

Slowly he opened the gate and went out. He moved past the Hutchinsons' house, past the Tennents', past the Weiceks'. There was a breeze now, and the smell of the Weiceks' flowers filled the air. He walked past the next house and hesitated, suddenly confused. Then he started through the **vacant lot** by the Akers' house. In the darkness it looked to him like the field he and Sara had crossed earlier in the evening on their way to see the swans.

He crossed the vacant lot, entered the wooded area, and walked slowly through the trees. He was certain that in just a moment he would come **into the clearing** and see the lake and the white swans gliding on the dark water. He continued walking, looking ahead so that he would see the lake as soon as possible.

The ground was getting rougher. There were stones to stumble over now and rain gullies and unexpected piles of trash. Still the thought of the swans **persisted** in his mind and he kept walking.

....

vacant lot empty land
into the clearing to the end of the trees
persisted stayed

Charlie cannot find the lake. He hears dogs in the distance and begins to run. Soon, he is lost and alone in the dark.

Chapter Ten

Charlie was getting tired and he knew something was wrong. The lake was gone. He paused and scanned the field, but he could not see anything familiar.

He turned to the right and began to walk up the hill. Suddenly a dog barked behind him. The sound, unexpected and loud, startled him, and he fell back a step and then started to run. Then another dog was barking, and another, and he had no idea where the dogs were. He was terribly frightened and he ran **with increasing awkwardness, thrashing at the weeds with his hands**, pulling at the air, so that everything about him seemed to be running except his slow feet.

The sound of the dogs seemed to him to be everywhere, all around him, so that he ran first in one

....

with increasing awkwardness, thrashing at the weeds with his hands pushing the weeds in a clumsy way direction, then in another, like a wild animal caught in a maze. He ran into a bush and the briers stung his face and arms, and he thought this was somehow connected with the dogs and thrashed his arms out wildly, not even feeling the cuts in his skin.

He turned around and around, trying to free himself, and then staggered on, running and pulling at the air. The dogs' barking **had grown fainter now, but in his terror** he did not notice. He ran blindly, stumbling over bushes and against trees, catching his clothing on twigs, kicking at unseen rocks. Then he came into a clearing and was able to **gain speed** for the first time.

He ran for a long way, and then suddenly he came up against a wire fence that cut him sharply across the chest. The surprise of it threw him back on the ground, and he sat holding his hands across his bare chest, gasping for breath.

Far down the hill someone had spoken to the dogs; they had grown quiet, and now there was only the rasping sound of Charlie's own breathing. He sat hunched over until his breathing grew quieter, and then he straightened and noticed his torn pajamas for the first time since he

....

had grown fainter now, but in his terror was far away now, but he was so afraid that

gain speed run faster

had left the house. He wrapped the frayed edges of the jacket carefully over his chest as if that would soothe the stinging cut.

After a while he got slowly to his feet, paused, and then began walking up the hill beside the fence. He was limping now because when he had fallen he had lost one of his bedroom slippers.

The fence ended abruptly. It was an old one, built long ago, and now only parts remained. Seeing it gone, Charlie felt relieved. It was as if the fence had kept him from his goal, and he stepped over a trailing piece of wire and walked toward the forest beyond.

Being in the trees gave him a good feeling for a while. The moonlight coming through the leaves and the soft sound of the wind in the branches were soothing, but as he went deeper into the forest he became worried. There was something here he didn't know, an unfamiliar smell, noises he had never heard before. He stopped.

He stood beneath the trees without moving and looked around him. He did not know where he was. He did not even know **how he had come to be there**. The whole night seemed one long struggle, but he could not remember why

....

how he had come to be there how he had gotten there

he had been struggling. He had wanted something, he could not remember what.

His face and arms stung from the brier scratches; his bare foot, tender and unused to walking on the rough ground, was already cut and sore, but most of all he **was gripped by hopelessness**. He wanted to be back in his room, in his bed, but home seemed **lost forever**, a place so disconnected from the forest that there was no way to get from one to the other.

He put his wrist to his ear and listened to his watch. Even its steady ticking could not help him tonight and he wrapped the torn pajamas tighter over his chest and began to walk slowly up the hill through the trees. As he walked, he began to cry without noise.

....

was gripped by hopelessness felt like he would never find his home

lost forever so far away

BEFORE YOU MOVE ON...

1. **Cause and Effect** Reread page 60. Charlie had been told never to go out of the yard. What caused him to go this time?

2. **Character's Point of View** Why did Charlie like being alone outside? What made his feelings change?

LOOK AHEAD Read pages 66–76 to find out how Sara tries to find Charlie.

The next morning, Aunt Willie and Sara cannot find Charlie. Sara thinks that he went to see the swans. She and Mary go to look.

Chapter Eleven

In the morning Sara **arose** slowly, letting her feet hang over the edge of the bed for a moment before she stepped onto the floor. Then she walked across the room, and as she passed the dressing table she paused to look at herself in the mirror. She smoothed her hair behind her ears.

One of her greatest mistakes, she thought, **looking at herself critically**, was cutting her hair. She had gone to the beauty school in Bentley, taking with her a picture from a magazine, and had asked the girl to cut her hair exactly like that.

"And look what she did to me!" she had screamed when she got home. "Look! **Ruined!**"

....

arose got out of bed

looking at herself critically looking in the mirror to see what was wrong

Ruined! It looks terrible!

"It's not that bad," Wanda had said.

"Tell the truth. Now look at that picture. Look! Tell the truth—do I look anything, anything at *all*, even the tiniest little bit, like that model?"

Wanda and Aunt Willie had had to admit that Sara looked nothing like the blond model.

"I'm ruined, just ruined. Why someone cannot take a perfectly good magazine picture and cut someone's hair the same way without ruining them is something I cannot understand. I hope that girl fails beauty school."

"Actually, your *hair* does sort of look like the picture. It's your face and body that don't."

"Shut up, Wanda. Quit trying to be funny."

"I'm not being funny. It's a fact."

"I didn't **make smart remarks the time they gave you that awful permanent**."

"You did too. You called me Gentle Ben."

"Well, I meant that as a compliment."

"All right, girls, stop this now. No more arguing. Believe me, I mean it."

Sara now looked at herself, **weighing the mistake of the hair**, and she thought suddenly: I look exactly like

....

make smart remarks the time they gave you that awful permanent say anything mean when they styled your hair badly

weighing the mistake of the hair thinking about what a mistake it was to cut her hair

that cartoon cat who is always chasing Tweetie Bird and who has just been run over by a steam roller and made absolutely flat. This hair and my flat face have combined to make me look exactly like—

"Sara!" Aunt Willie called from the kitchen.

"What?"

"Come on and get your breakfast, you and Charlie. I'm not going to be in here fixing one breakfast after another until lunch time."

"All right."

She went into the hall and looked into Charlie's room. "Charlie!"

He was not in his bed. She walked into the living room. Lately, since he had learned to turn on the television, he would get up early, come in, and watch it by himself, but he was not there either.

"Charlie's already up, Aunt Willie."

In the kitchen Aunt Willie was spooning oatmeal into two bowls.

"Oatmeal again," Sara groaned. "I believe I'll just have some Kool-Aid and toast."

"**Don't talk nonsense.** Now, where's Charlie?"

"He wasn't in his room."

....

Don't talk nonsense. Do not be silly; Stop joking.

She sighed. "Well, find him."

"First I've got to see my shoes." She went over to the sink and looked at the sneakers. "Oh, they look awful. Look at them, Aunt Willie. They're gross."

"Well, you should have left them alone. I've learned my lesson about dyeing clothes, let me tell you. You saw me, I hope, when I had to wear that purple dress to your Uncle Bert's funeral."

"What color would you say these were?"

"I haven't got time for that now. Go get your brother."

"No, there's a name for this color. I just want to see if you know it."

"I don't know it, so go get your brother."

"I'll give you three choices. It's either, let me see—it's either pomegranate, Pomeranian, or puce."

"Puce. Now go get your brother."

"How did you know?"

"Because my aunt had twin Pomeranian dogs that rode in a baby carriage and because I once ate a piece of pomegranate. Go get your brother!"

Sara put down the shoes and went back into the hall. "Charlie!" She looked into his room again. "Oh, Charlie!" She went out onto the front porch and looked at Charlie's

....

"What color would you say these were?" "What color are these?"

tent. It had blown down during the night and she could see that he wasn't there.

Slowly she walked back through the hall, looking into every room, and then into the kitchen.

"I can't find him, Aunt Willie."

"What do you mean, you can't find him?" Aunt Willie, **prepared to chide** the two children for being late to breakfast, now set the pan of oatmeal down heavily on the table.

"He's not in his room, he's not in the yard, he's not anywhere."

"If this is some kind of a joke—" Aunt Willie began. She brushed past Sara and went into the living room. "Charlie! Where are you, Charlie?" **Her voice had begun to rise with the sudden alarm** she often felt in connection with Charlie. "Where could he have gone?" She turned and looked at Sara. "If this is a joke . . . "

"It's not a joke."

"Well, I'm remembering **last April Fool's Day**, that's all."

"He's probably around the neighborhood somewhere, like the time Wanda took him to the store without saying

....

prepared to chide who was ready to yell at

Her voice had begun to rise with the sudden alarm She started to sound worried, the way

last April Fool's Day the last time time you tried to trick me

anything."

"Well, Wanda didn't take him this morning." Aunt Willie walked into the hall and stood looking in Charlie's room. She stared at the empty bed. She did not move for a moment as she tried to think of **some logical explanation for his absence**. "If anything's happened to that boy—"

"Nothing's happened to him."

"All right, where is he?"

Sara did not answer. Charlie had never left the house alone, and Sara could not think of any place he could be either.

"Go outside, Sara. Look! If he's not in the neighborhood, I'm calling the police."

"Don't call until we're sure, Aunt Willie, please."

"I'm calling. Something's wrong here."

Sara was out of her pajamas and into her pants and shirt in a minute. Leaving her pajamas on the floor, she ran barefoot into the yard.

"Charlie! Charlie!" She ran around the house and then stopped. Suddenly she remembered the swans and ran back into the house.

"Aunt Willie, **I bet you anything** Charlie went down

....

some logical explanation for his absence a reason why
Charlie was gone

I bet you anything I'm sure that

to the lake to see the swans."

Aunt Willie was talking on the telephone and she put one hand over the receiver and said, "Run and see."

"You aren't talking to the police already?" Sara asked in the doorway.

"I'm not talking to the police, but that's what I'm going to do when you get back. **Now quit wasting time.**"

"Just let me get my shoes."

She ran back into the kitchen and put on the sneakers, which were still wet. Then she ran out of the house and down the street. As she passed the Weiceks', Mary came out on the porch.

"**What's the hurry?**" she called.

"Charlie's missing. I'm going to see if he's down at the lake."

"I'll go with you." She came down the steps, calling over her shoulder, "Mom, I'm going to help Sara look for Charlie."

"**Not in those curlers you're not.**"

"Mom, I've got on a scarf. Nobody can even tell it's rolled."

"Yeah, everyone will just think you have real bumpy

Now quit wasting time. Hurry up.

What's the hurry? Why are you running?

"Not in those curlers you're not." "You can't leave when you're wearing curlers in your hair."

hair," Sara said.

"Oh, hush. Now what's all this about Charlie?"

"We couldn't find him this morning and I think he might have got up during the night and gone to see the swans. He acted awful when we had to leave."

"I know. I saw you dragging him up the street last night."

"I had to. It was the only way I could get him home. It was **black dark**. You couldn't even see the swans and he still wouldn't come home."

"I hope he's all right."

"He's probably sitting down there looking at the swans, holding onto the grass, and I'm going to have to drag him up the hill screaming all over again. He's strong when he wants to be, you know that?"

"Hey, you've got your shoes on."

"Yeah, but they're still wet."

"You'll probably have puce feet before the day's over."

"That's all I need."

They turned and crossed the field at the bottom of the hill.

"Let's hurry because **Aunt Willie is at this moment**

···

black dark really dark
Aunt Willie is at this moment I know Aunt Willie is

getting ready to call the police."

"Really?"

"She's sitting by the phone now. She's got her little card out with all **her emergency numbers** on it and her finger is pointing right to *POLICE*."

"Remember that time the old man got lost in the woods? What was his name?"

"Uncle somebody."

"And they **organized a posse of college boys** and the Red Cross brought coffee and everything, and then they found the old man asleep in his house the next morning. He was on a picnic and had got bored and just went home."

"Don't remind me. Probably as soon as Aunt Willie calls the police we'll find Charlie in the bathroom or somewhere."

They came through the trees and into the clearing around the lake. Neither spoke.

"Yesterday he was sitting right here," Sara said finally. "Charlie! Charlie!"

There was no answer, but the swans turned abruptly

....

her emergency numbers the telephone numbers she uses when she needs help

organized a posse of college boys found a group of college boys to search for the man

and began to glide to the other side of the lake. Sara felt her shoulders sag and she **rammed** her hands into her back pockets.

"Something really has happened to him," she said. "I know it now."

"Probably not, Sara."

"I *know* it now. Sometimes you just know terrible things. I get a feeling in my neck, like my shoulders **have come unhinged** or something, when an awful thing happens."

Mary put one hand on her arm. "Maybe he's hiding somewhere."

"He can't even do that right. If he's playing hide-and-seek, as soon as he's hidden he starts looking out to see how the game's going. He just can't—"

"Maybe he's at the store or up at the Dairy Queen. I could **run up to** the drugstore."

"No, something's happened to him."

They stood at the edge of the water. Sara looked at the swans without seeing them.

Mary called, "Charlie! Charlie!" Her kerchief slipped

....

rammed put, shoved
have come unhinged are going to fall off
run up to go look in

off and she retied it over her rollers. "Charlie!"

"I was so sure he'd be here," Sara said. "I wasn't even worried because I knew he would be sitting right here. Now I don't know what to do."

"Let's go back to the house. Maybe he's there now."

"I know he won't be."

"Well, don't **get discouraged until we see**." She took Sara by the arm and started walking through the trees. "You know who you sound like? Remember when Mary Louise **was up for** class president and she kept saying, 'I know I won't get it. I know I won't get it.' For three days that was all she said."

"And she didn't get it."

"Well, I just meant you sounded like her, your voice or something," Mary explained quickly. "Now, come on."

....

get discouraged until we see give up hope before we know more

was up for wanted to be

BEFORE YOU MOVE ON...

1. **Plot** Reread pages 73–74. Where did Sara go to find Charlie? Why did she think he was there?

2. **Inference** Reread pages 72–74. Why do you think Sara didn't want Aunt Willie to call the police?

LOOK AHEAD Read pages 77–85 to find out how Sara feels about Charlie.

Sara and Mary can't find Charlie. Aunt Willie calls the police. Sara remembers two times when she thought people had hurt Charlie.

Chapter Twelve

When Sara entered the house with Mary, Aunt Willie was still sitting at the telephone. She was saying, "And **there's not a trace of him**." She paused in her conversation to ask, "Did you find him?" and when Sara shook her head, she said into the telephone, "I'm hanging up now, Midge, so I can call the police. Sara just came in and he wasn't at the lake."

She hung up, took her card of emergency phone numbers and began to dial.

There was something final about calling the police and Sara said, "Aunt Willie, don't call yet. Maybe—"

"I'm calling. **A hundred elephants couldn't stop me.**"

"Maybe he's at somebody's house," Mary said.

···

there's not a trace of him no one knows where he is

There was something final about calling the police
Calling the police made her scared and worried

A hundred elephants couldn't stop me. Nothing is going to stop me.

"One time my brother went in the Hutchinsons' to watch TV and we—"

"Hello, is this the police department? I want to **report a missing child**."

She looked up at Sara, started to say something, then turned back to her telephone conversation. "Yes, a missing child, a boy, ten, Charlie Godfrey. G-o-d-f-r-e-y." Pause. "Eighteen-oh-eight Cass Street. This is Willamina Godfrey, his aunt. **I'm in charge**." She paused, then said, "Yes, since last night." She listened again. "No, I don't know what time. We woke up this morning, he was gone. That's all." She listened and as she answered again her voice began to **rise with concern and anger**. "No, I could not ask his friends about him because he doesn't have any friends. His brain was injured when he was three years old and that is why I am so concerned. This is not a ten-year-old boy who can go out and come home when he feels like it. This is not a boy who's going to run out and break street lights and spend the night in some garage, if that's what you're thinking. This is a boy, I'm telling you, who can be lost and afraid three blocks from home and cannot speak one word to ask for help. Now are you going to

....

report a missing child tell you that my child is lost
I'm in charge. I take care of the children.
rise with concern and anger sound worried and angry

come out here or aren't you?"

She paused, said, "Yes, yes," then grudgingly, "And thank you." She hung up the receiver and looked at Sara. "They're coming."

"What did they say?"

"They said they're coming. That's all." She rose **in agitation** and began to walk into the living room. "Oh, why don't they hurry!"

"Aunt Willie, they just hung up the telephone."

"I know." She went to the front door and then came back, nervously slapping her hands together. "Where can he *be*?"

"My brother was always getting lost when he was little," Mary said.

"I stood right in this house, in that room," Aunt Willie interrupted. She pointed toward the front bedroom. "And I promised your mother, Sara, that I would look after Charlie **all my life**. I promised your mother nothing would ever happen to Charlie as long as there was breath in my body, and now look. Look! Where is this boy I'm taking such good care of?" She threw her hands into the air. "**Vanished without a trace**, that's where."

....

in agitation feeling scared and worried

all my life forever

Vanished without a trace He is gone, and I have no idea where he is

"Aunt Willie, you can't watch him every minute."

"Why not? Why can't I? What have I got more important in my life than looking after that boy? Only one thing more important than Charlie. Only one thing—that devil television there."

"Aunt Willie—"

"Oh, yes, that devil television. I was sitting right in that chair last night and he wanted me to sew on one button for him but I was too busy with the television. I'll tell you what I should have told your mother six years ago. I should have told her, 'Sure, I'll be glad to look after Charlie except when there's something good on television. I'll be glad to watch him **in my spare time**.' My tongue should fall out on the floor for promising to look after your brother and not doing it."

She went back to the doorway. "There are a hundred things that could have happened to him. He could have fallen into one of those **ravines** in the woods. He could be lost up at the old mine. He could be at the bottom of the lake. He could be kidnaped." Sara and Mary stood in silence as she named the **tragedies that could have befallen** Charlie.

....

in my spare time when I have nothing else to do

ravines deep valleys

tragedies that could have befallen bad things that could have happened to

Sara said, "Well, he could not have been kidnaped, because anybody would know we don't have any money for ransom."

"That wouldn't stop some people. Where are those policemen?"

Sara looked down at the table beside the television and saw a picture Charlie had drawn of himself on tablet paper. The head and body were circles of the same size, the ears and eyes overlapping smaller circles, the arms and legs were elongated balloons. He had started printing his name below the picture, but had completed only two letters before he had gone out to make the tent. The C was backward.

Wanda had bought him the tablet and crayons two days ago and he had done this one picture with the brown crayon. It gave Sara a sick feeling to see it because something about the picture, the smallness, the unfinished quality, made it look somehow **very much** like Charlie.

Aunt Willie said, "When you want the police they are always a hundred miles away bothering criminals."

"**They're on their way.** They said so," Mary said.

....

very much a lot
They're on their way. They are coming here now.

"All right then, where are they?"

Mary blinked her eyes at this question to which she had no answer, and settled the rollers beneath her scarf.

"I still can't get it out of my head that Charlie went back to see the swans," Sara said.

"He really was upset about having to go home. **I can testify to that**," Mary said.

Aunt Willie left the room abruptly. When she came back she was holding a picture of Charlie in one hand. It was a snapshot of him taken in March, sitting on the steps with Boysie in front of the house.

"The police always want a photograph," she said. She held it out so Mary and Sara could see it. "Mrs. Hutchinson took that with her Polaroid."

"It's a real good picture of him," Mary said.

Sara looked at the picture without speaking. Somehow the awkward, unfinished crayon drawing on the table looked more like Charlie than the snapshot.

"It was his birthday," Aunt Willie said **mournfully**, "and look how proud he was of that watch Wanda bought him, holding his little arm straight out in the picture so everyone would notice it. I fussed so much about Wanda getting him a watch because he couldn't tell time, and

....

I can testify to that I saw him myself
mournfully in a sad way

then he was so proud just to be wearing it. Everyone would ask him on the street, 'What time is it, Charlie? Have you got the time, Charlie?' just to see how proud he was to show them."

"And then those boys stole it. I think that was the meanest thing," Mary said.

"The watch was lost," Aunt Willie said. "The watch just got lost."

"Stolen," Sara snapped, "by that crook Joe Melby."

"I am the quickest person to **accuse somebody**, you know that. You saw me, I hope, when I noticed those boys making off with the Hutchinsons' porch chairs last Halloween; but that watch just got lost. Then Joe Melby found it and, to his credit, brought it back."

"Huh!"

"There was no stealing involved."

Mary said, giggling, "Aunt Willie, did Sara ever tell you what she did to Joe?"

"Hush, Mary," Sara said.

"What did she do?"

"She made a little sign that said *FINK* and stuck it on Joe's back in the hall at school and he went around for two periods without knowing it was there."

....

accuse somebody say when someone does something wrong

"There was no stealing involved." "No one stole the watch."

"It doesn't matter what I did. Nobody's going to **pick on** my brother and I mean it. That fink stole Charlie's watch and then got scared and told that big lie about finding it on the floor of the school bus."

"You want revenge too much."

"When somebody *deserves* revenge, then—"

"I take my revenge same as anybody," Aunt Willie said, "only I never was one to **keep after somebody and keep after somebody** the way you do. You take after your Uncle Bert in that."

"I hope I always do."

"No, your Uncle Bert was no good in that way. He would never **let a grudge leave him**. When he lay dying in the hospital, he was telling us who we weren't to speak to and who we weren't to do business with. His dying words were against Jeep Johnson at the used-car lot."

"Good for Uncle Bert."

"And that nice little Gretchen Wyant who you turned the hose on, and her wearing a silk dress her brother had sent her from Taiwan!"

"That nice little Gretchen Wyant was lucky all

....

pick on tease

keep after somebody and keep after somebody keep trying to punish people

let a grudge leave him forgive someone who had made him angry

84

she got was water on her silk dress."

"Sara!"

"Well, do you know what that nice little Gretchen Wyant did? I was standing in the bushes by the spigot, turning off the hose, and this nice little Gretchen Wyant didn't see me—all she saw was Charlie at the fence—and she said, 'How's the *retard* today?' only she made it sound even uglier, 'How's the *reeeeetard*,' like that. Nothing ever made me so mad. The best sight of my whole life was nice little Gretchen Wyant standing there in her wet Taiwan silk dress with her mouth hanging open."

"Here come the police," Mary said quickly. "But they're stopping next door."

"Signal to them," Aunt Willie said.

Before Mary could move to the door, Aunt Willie was past her and out on the porch. "Here we are. This is the house." She turned and said over her shoulder to Sara, **"Now, God willing, we'll get some action."**

....

she got was I did was throw

**Now, God willing, we'll
get some action.** Now I
hope they will help us.

BEFORE YOU MOVE ON...

1. **Comparisons** Reread page 81. Describe Charlie's drawing. Why did the drawing make Sara feel sick?

2. **Character** What did Sara do when people teased Charlie? What does that show about Sara?

LOOK AHEAD Read pages 86–93 to find out more about Sara's father.

Aunt Willie thinks that Sara's father will come when he hears that Charlie is missing. Sara is not so sure.

Chapter Thirteen

Sara sat in the living room wearing her cut-off blue jeans, an old shirt with *Property of State Prison* **stamped** on the back which Wanda had brought her from the beach, and her puce tennis shoes. She was sitting in the doorway, leaning back against the door with her arms wrapped around her knees, listening to Aunt Willie, who was making a telephone call in the hall.

"**It's no use calling**," Sara said against her knees. This was the first summer her knees had not been skinned a dozen times, but she could still see the white scars from other summers. Since Aunt Willie did not answer, she said again, "It's no use calling. He won't come."

"You don't know your father," Aunt Willie said.

"**That is the truth.**"

"Not like I do. When he hears that Charlie is missing,

---

stamped written

It's no use calling You don't need to call

"That is the truth." "You are right. I do not know him."

he will . . . " Her voice trailed off as she prepared to dial the telephone.

Sara had a strange feeling when she thought of her father. It was the way she felt about people she didn't know well, like the time Miss Marshall, her English teacher, had given her a ride home from school, and Sara had felt uneasy the whole way home, even though she saw Miss Marshall everyday.

Her father's remoteness had begun, she thought, with Charlie's illness. There was a picture in the family photograph album of her father laughing and throwing Sara into the air and a picture of her father holding her on his shoulders and a picture of her father sitting on the front steps with Wanda on one knee and Sara on the other. All these pictures of a happy father and his adoring daughters had been taken before Charlie's illness and Sara's mother's death. Afterward there weren't any family pictures at all, happy or sad.

When Sara looked at those early pictures, she remembered a laughing man with black curly hair and a broken tooth who had lived with them for a few short **golden** years and then had gone away. There was no

....

Her father's remoteness had begun, she thought, with Charlie's illness. Her father had started spending less time with the family after Charlie got sick.

golden happy

connection at all between this laughing man in the photograph album and the gray sober man who worked in Ohio and came home to West Virginia on occasional weekends, who sat in the living room and watched baseball or football on television and never started a conversation on his own.

Sara listened while Aunt Willie explained to the operator that the call she was making was an emergency. "That's why I'm not **direct dialing**," she said, "because I'm so upset I'll get the wrong numbers."

"He won't come," Sara whispered against her knee.

As the operator put through the call and Aunt Willie waited, she turned to Sara, nodded emphatically, and said, "He'll come, you'll see."

Sara got up, walked across the living room and into the kitchen, where the breakfast dishes were still on the table. She looked down at the two bowls of hard, cold oatmeal, and then made herself three pieces of toast and poured herself a cup of cherry Kool-Aid. When she came back eating the toast Aunt Willie was still waiting.

"Didn't the operator tell them it was an emergency, I wonder," Aunt Willie said impatiently.

"Probably."

----

direct dialing dialing the numbers myself

"Well, if somebody told me I had an emergency call, I would run, let me tell you, to find out what that emergency was. That's no breakfast, Sara."

"It's my lunch."

"Kool-Aid and toast will not **sustain you** five minutes." She broke off quickly and said in a louder voice, "Sam, is that you?" She nodded to Sara, then turned back to the telephone, bent forward in her concern. "First of all, Sammy, promise me you won't get upset—no, promise me first."

"He won't get upset. Even *I* can promise you that," Sara said with her mouth full of toast.

"Sam, Charlie's missing," Aunt Willie said abruptly.

Unable to listen to any more of the conversation, Sara took her toast and went out onto the front porch. She sat on the front steps and put her feet into the worn grooves that Charlie's feet had made on the third step. Then she ate the last piece of toast and licked the butter off her fingers.

In the corner of the yard, beneath the elm tree, she could see the hole Charlie had dug with a spoon; all one morning he had dug that hole and now Boysie was lying

....

sustain you make you feel full for more than

in it for coolness. She walked to the tree and sat in the old rope swing and swung over Boysie. She stretched out her feet and touched Boysie, and he lifted his head and looked around to see who had poked him, then lay back in his hole.

"Boysie, here I am, look, Boysie, look."

He was already asleep again.

"Boysie—" She looked up as Aunt Willie came out on the porch and stood for a minute drying her hands on her apron. **For the occasion of Charlie's disappearance she** was wearing her best dress, a bright green bonded jersey, which was so hot her face above it was red and shiny. Around her forehead she had tied a handkerchief to absorb the sweat.

Sara swung higher. "Well," she asked, "is he coming?" She paused to pump herself higher. "Or not?"

"He's going to call back tonight."

"Oh," Sara said.

"Don't say 'Oh' to me like that."

"It's what I figured."

"Listen to me, Miss Know-it-all. There is no need in the world for your father to come **this exact minute**. If he

....

For the occasion of Charlie's disappearance she Because Charlie had disappeared, Aunt Willie

"It's what I figured." "I knew he would do that."

this exact minute right now

started driving right this second he still wouldn't get here till after dark and he couldn't do anything then, so he just might as well wait till after work and then drive."

"Might as well do the sensible thing." Sara stood up and really began to swing. She had grown so much taller since she had last stood in this swing that her head came almost to the limb from which the swing hung. She caught hold of the limb with her hands, kicked her feet free, and let the swing jerk wildly on its own.

"Anyway," Aunt Willie said, "this is no time to be playing on a swing. What will the neighbors think, with Charlie missing and you having a wonderful time on a swing?"

"I knew he wouldn't come."

"He is going to come," Aunt Willie said in a louder voice. "He is just going to wait till dark, which is reasonable, since by dark Charlie will probably be home anyway."

"It is so reasonable that it makes me sick."

"I won't listen to you **being disrespectful to** your father, I mean that," she said. "I know what it is **to lose a father**, let me tell you, and so will you when all you have

....

"Might as well do the sensible thing." "He should do what is easiest for him."

being disrespectful to say rude things about

to lose a father to not have a father

left of him is an envelope."

Aunt Willie, Sara knew, was speaking of the envelope in her dresser drawer containing all the things her father had had in his pockets when he died. Sara knew them all—the watch, the twenty-seven cents in change, the folded dollar bill, the brown plaid handkerchief, the three-cent stamp, the two bent pipe cleaners, the half pack of stomach mints.

"Yes, wait till you lose your father. Then you'll **appreciate him**."

"I've already lost him."

"Don't you talk like that. Your father's had to raise two families and all by himself. When Poppa died, Sammy had to go to work and support all of us before he was even out of high school, and now he's got this family to support, too. It's not easy, I'm telling you that. *You* raise two families and then I'll listen to what you've got to say against your father."

Sara let herself drop to the ground and said, "I better go. Mary and I are going to look for Charlie."

"Where?"

"Up the hill."

"Well, don't *you* get lost," Aunt Willie called after her.

---

appreciate him know how important he was to you

From the Hutchinsons' yard some children called, "Have you found Charlie yet, Sara?" They were making a garden in the dust, carefully planting flowers without roots in neat rows. Already the first flowers were beginning to **wilt** in the hot sun.

"I'm going to look for him now."

"Sawa?" It was the youngest Hutchinson boy, who was three and sometimes came over to play with Charlie.

"What?"

"Sawa?"

"What?"

"Sawa?"

"*What?*"

"Sawa, I got gwass." He held up two fists of grass he had just pulled from one of the few remaining clumps in the yard.

"Yes, that's fine. I'll tell Charlie when I see him."

....

wilt die

BEFORE YOU MOVE ON...

1. **Comparisons** Reread page 87. What was Sara's father like before Charlie's illness? How did he change?

2. **Inference** What did Sara mean when she said that she "already lost" her father?

LOOK AHEAD Read pages 94–105 to find out what happens when Sara talks to Joe.

Sara is on her way to Mary's house when she meets Joe Melby. He offers to help her find Charlie. Sara doesn't want his help.

Chapter Fourteen

Sara and Mary had decided that they would go to the lake and walk up behind the houses toward the woods. Sara was now on her way to Mary's, passing the vacant lot where **a baseball game was in progress**. She glanced up and watched as she walked down the sidewalk.

The baseball game had been going on for an hour with the score still zero to zero and the players, dusty and tired, were playing silently, without hope.

She was almost past the field when she heard someone call, "Hey, have you found your brother yet, Sara?"

She recognized the voice of Joe Melby and said, "No," without looking at him.

"What?"

She turned, **looked directly at him**, and said, "You

....

a baseball game was in progress people were playing baseball
looked directly at him looked at his face

will be **pleased and delighted to learn** that we have not."
She continued walking down the street. The blood began
to pound in her head. Joe Melby was the one person she
did not want to see on this particular day. There was
something disturbing about him. She did not know him,
really, had hardly even spoken to him, and yet she hated
him so much the sight of him made her sick.

"**Is there anything I can do?**"

"No."

"If he's up in the woods, I could help look. I know
about as much about those hills as anybody." He left the
game and started walking behind her with his hands in
his pockets.

"No, thank you."

"I *want* to help."

She swirled around and faced him, her eyes blazing.
"I do not want your help." They looked at each other.
Something twisted inside her and she felt suddenly ill. She
thought she would never drink cherry Kool-Aid again as
long as she lived.

Joe Melby did not say anything but moved one foot
back and forth on the sidewalk, shuffling at some sand.

....

pleased and delighted to learn happy to hear
"Is there anything I can do?" "Can I help you?"

"Do you—"

"Anybody who would steal a little boy's watch," she said, cutting off his words, and **it was a relief to make this accusation to his face at last**, "is somebody whose help **I can very well do without**." Her head was pounding so loudly she could hardly hear her own words. For months, ever since the incident of the stolen watch, she had waited for this moment, had planned exactly what she would say. Now that it was said, she did not feel **the triumph** she had imagined at all.

"Is that what's wrong with you?" He looked at her. "You think I stole your brother's watch?"

"I know you did."

"How?"

"Because I asked Charlie who stole his watch and I kept asking him and one day on the school bus when I asked him he pointed right straight at you."

"He was confused—"

"He wasn't that confused. You probably thought he wouldn't be able to tell on you because he couldn't talk, but he pointed right—"

"He *was* confused. I gave the watch *back* to him.

....

it was a relief to make this accusation to his face at last
she was glad to tell him what she thought

I can very well do without I do not need

the triumph as happy as

I didn't take it."

"I don't believe you."

"You believe what you want then, but I didn't take that watch. I thought **that matter had been settled**."

"Huh!"

She turned and started walking with great speed down the hill. For some reason she was not as sure about Joe Melby as she had been before, and this was even more disturbing. He did take the watch, she said to herself. She could not bear to think that she **had been mistaken in this**, that she had taken revenge on the wrong person.

Behind her there were sudden cheers as someone hit a home run. The ball went into the street. Joe ran, picked it up, and tossed it to a boy in the field. Sara did not look around.

"Hey, wait a minute," she heard Joe call. "I'm coming."

She did not turn around. **She had fallen into that trap before.** Once when she had been walking down the street, she had heard a car behind her and the horn sounding and a boy's voice shouting, "Hey, beautiful!" And she had turned around. She! Then, too late, she had seen that the girl they were honking and shouting at was Rosey

....

that matter had been settled everyone already knew the truth
had been mistaken in this was wrong about this
She had fallen into that trap before. She had made the same mistake before.

Camdon on the opposite side of the street, Rosey Camdon who was Miss Batelle District Fair and Miss Buckwheat Queen and a hundred other things. Sara had looked down quickly, not knowing whether anyone had seen her or not, and her face had **burned so fiercely** she had thought it would be red forever. Now she kept walking quickly with her head down.

"Wait, Sara."

Still she did not turn around or show that she had heard him.

"Wait." He ran, caught up with her, and started walking beside her. "All the boys say they want to help."

She hesitated but kept walking. She could not think of anything to say. She knew how circus men on stilts felt when they walked, because her legs seemed to be moving in the same awkward way, **great exaggerated steps that got her nowhere**.

She thought she might start crying so she said quickly, "Oh, all right." Then tears did come to her eyes, sudden and hot, and she looked down at her feet.

He said, "Where should we start? Have you got any ideas?"

....

burned so fiercely turned so red that

great exaggerated steps that got her nowhere trying hard to walk, but not moving far

"I think he's up in the woods. I took him to see the swans yesterday and I think he was looking for them when he got lost."

"Probably up that way."

She nodded.

He paused, then added, "We'll find him."

She did not answer, could not, because **tears were spilling down her cheeks**, so she turned quickly and walked alone to Mary's house and waited on the sidewalk until Mary came out to join her.

....

tears were spilling down her cheeks she was crying

Mary and Sara go to look for Charlie. Mary tells Sara the truth about Charlie's watch and Sara learns something about herself.

Chapter Fifteen

She and Mary were almost across the open field before Sara spoke. Then she said, "Guess who just stopped me and **gave me the big sympathy talk** about Charlie."

"I don't know. Who?"

"Joe Melby."

"Really? What did he say?"

"He wants to help look for Charlie. **He makes me sick.**"

"I think it's nice that he wants to help."

"Well, maybe if he'd stolen your brother's watch you wouldn't think it was so nice."

Mary was silent for a moment. Then she said, "I probably shouldn't tell you this, but he didn't steal that watch, Sara."

....

gave me the big sympathy talk said that he was sorry

He makes me sick. I don't like him at all.

"Huh!"

"No, he really didn't."

Sara looked at her and said, "How do you know?"

"I can't tell you how I know because I promised I wouldn't, but I *know* he didn't."

"How?"

"I can't tell. I promised."

"**That never stopped you before.** Now, Mary Weicek, you tell me what you know this minute."

"I promised."

"Mary, tell me."

"**Mom would kill me** if she knew I told you."

"She won't know."

"Well, your aunt went to see Joe Melby's mother."

"What?"

"Aunt Willie went over to see Joe Melby's mother."

"She didn't!"

"Yes, she did, too, because my mother was right there when it happened. It was about two weeks after Charlie had gotten the watch back."

"I don't believe you."

"Well, it's the truth. You told Aunt Willie that Joe had

....

That never stopped you before. You always told me things before.

Mom would kill me Mom would be angry

stolen the watch—remember, you told everybody—and so Aunt Willie went over to see Joe's mother."

"She wouldn't do such a terrible thing."

"Well, she did."

"And what did Mrs. Melby say?"

"She called Joe into the room and she said, 'Joe, did you steal the little Godfrey boy's watch?' And he said, 'No.'"

"What did you **expect him to say** in front of his mother? 'Yes, I stole the watch'? Huh! **That doesn't prove anything.**"

"So then she said, 'I want the truth now. Do you know who did take the watch?' and he said that nobody had *stolen* the watch."

"So where did it disappear to for a week, I'd like to know."

"I'm coming to that. He said some **of the fellows** were out in front of the drugstore and Charlie was standing there waiting for the school bus—you were in the drug store. Remember it was the day we were getting the stamps for letters to those pen pals who never answered? Remember the stamps wouldn't come out of the machine?

....

expect him to say think he would say

That doesn't prove anything. He could be lying.

of the fellows boys

Well, anyway, these boys outside the store started teasing Charlie with some candy, and while Charlie was trying to get the candy, one of the boys took off Charlie's watch without Charlie noticing it. Then they were going to ask Charlie what time it was and when he looked down at his watch, he would get upset because the watch would be gone. They were just going to tease him."

"Finks! *Finks!*"

"Only you came out of the drugstore right then and saw what they were doing with the candy and told them off and the bus came and you hustled Charlie on the bus before anybody had a chance to give back the watch. Then they got scared to give it back and that's the whole story. Joe didn't steal the watch at all. **He wasn't even in on it.** He came up right when you did and didn't even know what had happened. Later, when he found out, he got the watch back and gave it to Charlie, that's all."

"Why didn't you tell me before this?"

"Because I just found out about it at lunch. For four months my mother has known all about this thing and never mentioned it because she said it was **one of those things best forgotten.**"

....

He wasn't even in on it. He didn't know what was happening.
one of those things best forgotten in the past and was not important anymore

"Why did she tell you now?"

"That's the way my mom is. We were talking about Charlie at the dinner table, and suddenly she comes up with this. Like one time she casually mentioned that she had had a long talk with Mr. Homer about me. Mr. Homer, the principal! She went over there and they had a long discussion and she never mentioned it for a year."

"That is the worst thing Aunt Willie has ever done."

"Well, **don't let on that you know** or I'll be in real trouble."

"I won't, but honestly, I could just—"

"You promised."

"I know. You don't have to keep reminding me. It makes me feel terrible though, I can tell you that." She walked with her head bent forward. "Terrible! You know what I just did when I saw him?"

"What?"

"Accused him of stealing the watch."

"Sara, you didn't."

"I did too. I can't **help myself**. When I think somebody has done something mean to Charlie I can't forgive them. I want to keep after them and keep after them just like

---

don't let on that you know don't tell anyone what I said

help myself stop

Aunt Willie said. I even **sort of suspected** Joe Melby hadn't really taken that watch and I still kept on—"

"Shh! Be quiet a minute." Mary was carrying her transistor radio and she held it up between them. "Listen."

The announcer was saying: "We have a report of a missing child in the Cass section—ten-year-old Charlie Godfrey, who has been missing from his home since sometime last night. He is wearing blue pajamas and brown felt slippers, has a watch on one wrist and an identification bracelet with his name and address on the other. He is a mentally handicapped child who cannot speak and may **become alarmed when approached by a stranger.** Please notify the police immediately if you have seen this youngster."

The two girls looked at each other, then continued walking across the field in silence.

....

sort of suspected thought that maybe

become alarmed when approached by a stranger feel scared if he sees someone he doesn't know

BEFORE YOU MOVE ON...

1. **Inference** Reread pages 98–99. Why did Sara start to cry?

2. **Character** Reread page 104. How did Sara feel after Mary told her the truth about Charlie's watch? What did Sara learn about herself?

LOOK AHEAD Read pages 106–117 to find out why Sara thinks it will be hard to find Charlie.

Sara and Mary argue. Then they meet Joe, who has found a clue to help them find Charlie. Sara has something important to say to Joe.

Chapter Sixteen

Mary and Sara were up in the field by the woods. They had been searching for Charlie for an hour without finding a trace of him.

Mary said, "I don't care how I look. I am taking off this scarf. It must be a hundred degrees out here."

"Charlie!" Sara called as she had been doing from time to time. Her voice had begun to sound **strained, she had called** so often. "Charlie!"

"Sara, do you know where we are?" Mary asked after a moment.

"Of course. The lake's down there and the old shack's over there and you can see them as soon as we get up a little higher."

"*If* we get up a little higher," Mary said in a tired voice.

"You didn't have to come, you know."

---

strained, she had called tired because she had yelled his name

"I wanted to come, only I just want to make sure we don't get lost. I have to go to Bennie Hoffman's party tonight."

"I know. You told me ten times."

"So I don't want to get lost." Mary walked a few steps without speaking. "I still can't figure out why I was invited, because Bennie Hoffman hardly knows me. I've just seen him two times this whole summer at the pool. Why do you think he—"

"Come on, will you?"

"It seems useless, if you ask me, to just keep walking when we don't really know which way he went. Aunt Willie thinks he went in the old coal mine."

"I know, but she only thinks that because she **associates the mine with tragedy** because her uncle and brother were killed in that coal mine. But Charlie wouldn't go in there. Remember that time we went into the **Bryants' cellar** after they moved out, and he wouldn't even come in there because it was cold and dark and sort of scary."

"Yes, I do remember because I **sprained my ankle**

....

associates the mine with tragedy thinks that only bad things happen at the coal mine

Bryants' cellar room under the Bryants' house

sprained my ankle hurt my ankle

jumping down from the window and had to wait two hours while you looked through old *Life* magazines."

"I was not looking through old magazines."

"I could hear you. I was down there in that dark cellar with the rats and you were upstairs and I was yelling for help and you kept saying, 'I'm going for help right now,' and I could hear the pages turning and turning and turning."

"Well, I got you out, didn't I?"

"Finally."

Sara paused again. "Charlie! Charlie!" The girls waited in the high grass for an answer, then began to walk again. Mary said, "Maybe we should have waited for the others before we started looking. They're going to have a regular organized posse with everybody walking along together. There may be a helicopter."

"The longer we wait, the harder it will be to find him."

"Well, I've got to get home in time to bathe and **take my hair down**."

"I know. I *know*. You're going to Bennie Hoffman's party."

"You don't have to sound so mad about it. I didn't *ask*

....

take my hair down brush my hair

to be invited."

"I am not mad because you were invited to Bennie Hoffman's party. I **couldn't care less** about Bennie Hoffman's party. I'm just mad because you're **slowing me up** on this search."

"Well, if I'm slowing you up so much, then maybe I'll just go on home."

"That **suits me fine**."

They looked at each other without speaking. Between them the radio began announcing: "Volunteers are needed in the Cass area in the search for young Charlie Godfrey, who disappeared from his home sometime during the night. A search of the Cheat woods will begin at three o'clock this afternoon."

Mary said, "Oh, I'll keep looking. I'll try to walk faster."

Sara shrugged, turned, and started walking up the hill, followed by Mary. They came to the old fence that once separated the pasture from the woods. Sara walked slowly beside the fence. "Charlie!" she called.

"Would he come if he heard you, do you think?"

Sara nodded. "But if they get a hundred people out

....

couldn't care less don't care

slowing me up making me go slower

suits me fine sounds like a good idea to me

here **clomping** through the woods and **hollering**, he's not going to come. He'll be too scared. I know him."

"I don't see how you can be so sure he came up this way."

"I just know. There's something about me that makes me understand Charlie. It's like I know how he feels about things. Like sometimes I'll be walking down the street and I'll pass the jeweler's and I'll think that if Charlie were here he would want to stand right there and look at those watches all afternoon and I know right where he'd stand and how he'd put his hands up on the glass and how his face would look. And yesterday I knew he was going to love the swans so much that he wasn't ever going to want to leave. I know how he feels."

"You just think you do."

"No, I *know.* I was thinking about the sky one night and I was looking up at the stars and I was thinking about how the sky goes on and on forever, and I couldn't understand it no matter how long I thought, and finally **I got kind of nauseated** and right then I started thinking, Well, this is how Charlie feels about some things. You know how it makes him sick sometimes to try to print

....

clomping walking loudly
hollering yelling loudly
I got kind of nauseated I felt a little sick

letters for a long time and—"

"Look who's coming," Mary interrupted.

"Where?"

"In the trees, walking toward us. Joe Melby."

"You're lying. You're just trying to make me—"

"It is him. Look." She quickly began to tie her scarf over her rollers again. "And you talk about *me* needing eyeglasses."

"Cut across the field, quick!" Sara said. "No, wait, go under the fence. Move, will you, Mary, and leave that scarf alone. Get under the fence. **I am not going to face him.** I mean it."

"I am not going under any fence. Anyway, it would look worse for us to run away than to just walk by casually."

"I cannot walk by casually after what I said."

"Well, you're going to have to face him sometime, and **it might as well be now** when everyone feels sorry for you about your brother." She called out, "Hi, Joe, **having any luck**?"

He came up to them and held out a brown felt slipper and looked at Sara. "Is this Charlie's?"

··

I am not going to face him. I don't want to see him.

it might as well be now you should just do it

having any luck did you find anything

Sara looked at the familiar object and forgot the incident of the watch for a moment. "Where did you find it?"

"Right up there by the fence. I had just picked it up when I saw you."

She took the slipper and, holding it against her, said, "Oh, I *knew* he came up this way, but it's a relief to **have some proof of it**."

"I was just talking to Mr. Aker," Joe continued, "and he said he heard his dogs barking up here last night. He had them tied out by the shack and he thought maybe someone was **prowling around**."

"Probably Charlie," Mary said.

"That's what I figured. Somebody ought to go down to the gas station and tell the people. They're organizing **a big search** now and half of the men are planning to go up to the mine."

There was a pause and Mary said, "Well, I guess I could go, only I don't know whether I'll have time to get back up here." She looked at Joe. "I promised Bennie Hoffman I'd come to his party tonight. That's why my hair's in rollers."

....

have some proof of it know for sure
prowling around walking past the dogs at night
a big search people to look for Charlie

"Tell them I found the slipper about a half mile up behind the Akers' at the old fence," Joe said.

"Sure. Are you coming to Bennie's tonight?"

"Maybe."

"Come. It's going to be fun."

Sara cleared her throat and said, "Well, I think I'll get on with my search **if you two will excuse me**." She turned and started walking up the hill again. There seemed to be a long silence in which **even the sound of the cicadas in the grass was absent**. She thrashed at the high weeds with her tennis shoes and hugged Charlie's slipper to her.

"Wait a minute, Sara, I'll come with you," Joe Melby said.

He joined her and she nodded, still looking down at the slipper. There was a picture of an Indian chief stamped on the top of the shoe and there was a loneliness to the Indian's profile, even stamped crudely on the felt, that she had never noticed before.

She cleared her throat again. "There is just one thing I want to say." Her voice did not even sound familiar, a tape-recorded voice.

He waited, then said, **"Go ahead."**

....

if you two will excuse me so I will leave now

even the sound of the cicadas in the grass was absent
even the bugs were quiet

Go ahead. I'm listening.

She did not speak for a moment but continued walking noisily through the weeds.

"Go ahead."

"If you'll just wait a minute, I'm trying to think how to say this." The words she wanted to say—I'm sorry—would not come out at all.

They continued walking in silence and then Joe said, "You know, I was just reading an article about a **guru** over in India and he hasn't spoken a word in twenty-eight years. *Twenty-eight years* and he hasn't said one word in all that time. And everyone has been waiting all those years to hear what he's going to say when he finally does speak because it's supposed to be some great wise word, and I thought about this poor guy sitting there and for twenty-eight years he's been trying to think of something to say that would **be the least bit great** and he can't think of anything and he must be getting really desperate now. And every day it gets worse and worse."

"Is there supposed to be some sort of message in that story?"

"Maybe."

She smiled. "Well, I just wanted to say that I'm sorry."

....

guru wise teacher
be the least bit great sound important

She thought again that she was going to start crying and she said to herself, You are nothing but a big soft snail. Snail!

"That's all right."

"I just found out about Aunt Willie going to see your mother."

He shrugged. **"She didn't mean anything by it."**

"But it was a terrible thing."

"It wasn't all that bad. At least it was different to be accused of something I *didn't* do for a change."

"But to be called in like that in front of Aunt Willie and Mary's mother. No, it was terrible." She turned and walked into the woods.

"Don't worry about it. I'm tough. I'm indestructible. I'm like that coyote in 'Road Runner' who is always getting flattened and dynamited and crushed and in the next scene is strolling along, completely normal again."

"I just acted too hastily. That's one of my **main faults**."

"I do that, too."

"Not like me."

"Worse probably. Do you remember when we used to

....

"She didn't mean anything by it." "She did not want to hurt me."

main faults problems

get grammar-school report cards, and the grades would be on one part of the card, and on the other side would be personality things the teacher would check, like '**Does not accept criticism constructively**'?"

Sara smiled. "I always used to get a check on that one," she said.

"Who didn't? And then they had one, '**Acts impetuously and without consideration for others**,' or something like that, and one year I got a double check on that one."

"You didn't."

"Yes, I did. Second grade. Miss McLeod. I remember she told the whole class that this was the first year she had ever had to give double checks to any student, and everyone in the room was scared to open his report card to see if he had got the double checks. And when I opened mine, there they were, two sets of double checks, on acting impetuously and on not accepting criticism, and single checks on everything else."

"Were you **crushed**?"

....

Does not accept criticism constructively Does not like to be told that he is wrong

Acts impetuously and without consideration for others Does things without thinking about other people first

crushed upset

"Naturally."

"I thought you were so tough and indestructible."

"Well, I am"—he paused—"I think." He pointed to the left. "Let's go up this way."

She agreed with a nod and went ahead of him between the trees.

....

"Naturally." "Yes. Of course."

BEFORE YOU MOVE ON...

1. **Conclusions** Reread pages 109–110. Why did Sara believe that it would be hard for other people to find Charlie?

2. **Summarize** Reread pages 114–115. Sara told Joe that she was sorry. What did she learn about Joe?

LOOK AHEAD Read pages 118–127 to find out where Charlie has gone.

Charlie is cold, tired, and lost at the bottom of a ravine. When his watch stops, he starts to cry.

Chapter Seventeen

There was a ravine in the forest, a deep cut in the earth, and Charlie **had made his way into it through an early morning fog**. By chance, blindly stepping through the fog with his arms outstretched, he had managed to pick the one path that led into the ravine, and when the sun came out and the fog **burned away**, he could not find the way out.

All the ravine looked the same in the daylight, the high walls, the masses of weeds and wild berry bushes, the trees. He had wandered around for a while, following the little paths made by dirt washed down from the hillside, but finally he sat down on a log and stared straight ahead without seeing.

After a while he **roused enough** to wipe his hands over

....

had made his way into it through an early morning fog
had walked into it when he couldn't see

burned away disappeared

roused enough got enough energy

his cheeks where the tears and dirt had dried together and to rub his puffed eyelids. Then he looked down, saw his bare foot, put it on top of his slipper, and sat with his feet overlapped.

There was a dullness about him now. He had had so many scares, heard so many frightening noises, started at so many shadows, been hurt so often that **all his senses were worn to a flat hopelessness**. He would just sit here forever.

It was not the first time Charlie had been lost, but never before had **there been this finality**. He had become separated from Aunt Willie once at the county fair and had not even known he was lost until she had come bursting out of the crowd screaming, "Charlie, Charlie," and **enveloped** him. He had been lost in school once in the hall and could not find his way back to his room, and he had walked up and down the halls, frightened by all the strange children looking out of every door, until one of the boys was sent out to lead him to his room. But in all his life there had never been an experience like this one.

He bent over and looked down at his watch, his eyes

....

all his senses were worn to a flat hopelessness now he was just tired and hopeless

there been this finality it seemed like they would never find him

enveloped hugged

on the tiny red hand. For the first time he noticed it was no longer moving. Holding his breath in his concern, he brought the watch closer to his face. The hand was still. For a moment he could not believe it. He watched it closely, waiting. Still the hand did not move. He shook his hand back and forth, as if he were trying to shake the watch off his wrist. He had seen Sara do this to her watch.

Then he held the watch to his ear. It was silent. He had had the watch for five months and **never before had it failed him**. He had not even known it could fail. And now it was silent and still.

He put his hand over the watch, covering it completely. He waited. His breathing had begun to quicken again. His hand on the watch was almost clammy. He waited, then slowly, cautiously, he removed his hand and looked at the tiny red hand on the dial. It was motionless. The trick had not worked.

Bending over the watch, he looked closely at **the stem**. Aunt Willie always wound the watch for him every morning after breakfast, but he did not know how she did this. He took the stem in his fingers, pulled at it clumsily, then harder, and it came off. He looked at it. Then, as he attempted to put it back on the watch, it fell to the ground

....

never before had it failed him it had never stopped working

the stem the part that wound the watch

and was lost in the leaves.

A chipmunk ran in front of him and scurried up the bank. **Distracted for a moment**, Charlie got up and walked toward it. The chipmunk paused and then darted into a hole, leaving Charlie standing in the shadows trying to see where it had gone. He went closer to the bank and pulled at the leaves, but he could not even find the place among the roots where the chipmunk had disappeared.

Suddenly something seemed to explode within Charlie, and he began to cry noisily. He threw himself on the bank and began kicking, **flailing at the ground**, at the invisible chipmunk, at the silent watch. He wailed, **yielding in helplessness to his anguish,** and his piercing screams, uttered again and again, seemed to hang in the air so that they overlapped. His fingers tore at the tree roots and dug beneath the leaves and scratched, animal-like, at the dark earth.

His body sagged and he rolled down the bank and was silent. He looked up at the trees, his chest still heaving with sobs, his face strangely still. After a moment, his eyelids drooped and he fell asleep.

....

Distracted for a moment Forgetting about the watch
flailing at the ground hitting the ground
yielding in helplessness to his anguish feeling sad and helpless

Sara and Joe continue to search for Charlie.
Joe helps Sara climb a high hill where they can
look down at the valley.

Chapter Eighteen

"Charlie! Charlie!"

The only answer was the call of a bird in the branches overhead, one long tremulous whistle.

"He's **not even within hearing distance**," Sara said.

For the past hour she and Joe Melby had been walking deeper and deeper into the forest without pause, and now the trees were so thick that only small spots of sunlight found their way through **the heavy foliage**.

"Charlie, oh, Charlie!"

She waited, looking down at the ground.

Joe said, "You want to rest for a while?"

Sara shook her head. She suddenly wanted to see her brother so badly that her throat began to close. It was a tight feeling she got sometimes when she wanted

---

not even within hearing distance too far away to hear us
the heavy foliage all the plants

something, like the time she had had the measles and had wanted to see her father so much she couldn't even swallow. Now she thought that if she had a whole glass of ice water—and she was thirsty—she probably would not be able to drink a single drop.

"If you can make it a little farther, there's a place at the top of the hill where the strip mining is, and you can see the whole valley from there."

"I can make it."

"Well, we can rest first if—"

"I can make it."

She suddenly felt a little better. She thought that if she could stand up there on top of the hill and look down and see, somewhere in that huge green valley, a small plump figure in blue pajamas, **she would ask for nothing more in life**. She thought of the valley as a **relief map** where everything would be shiny and smooth, and her brother would be right where she could **spot him** at once. Her cry, "There he is!" would ring like a bell over the valley and everyone would hear her and know that Charlie had been found.

She paused, leaned against a tree for a moment, and

....

she would ask for nothing more in life she would be happy for the rest of her life

relief map big map of hills and valleys

spot him see him

then continued. Her legs had begun to tremble.

It was the time of afternoon when she usually sat down in front of the television and watched game shows, the shows where the married couples tried to guess things about each other and where girls had to **pick out dates** they couldn't see. She would sit in the doorway to the hall where she always sat and Charlie would come in and watch with her, and the living room would be dark and smell of the pine-scented cleaner Aunt Willie used.

Then "The Early Show" would come on, and she would sit through the old movie, leaning forward in the doorway, making fun, saying things like, "Now, Charlie, we'll have the old Convict Turning Honest scene," and Charlie, sitting on the stool closer to the television, would nod without understanding.

She was good, too, at joining in the dialogue with the actors. When the cowboy would say something like, "Things are quiet around here tonight," she would join in with, "Yeah, *too* quiet," right on cue. It seemed strange to be out here in the woods with Joe Melby instead of in the living room with Charlie, watching *Flame of Araby*, which was the early movie for that afternoon.

----

pick out dates choose partners

Her progress up the hill seemed slower and slower. It was like the time she had won the slow bicycle race, a race in which she had to go as slow as possible without letting a foot touch the ground, and she had gone slower and slower, **all the while feeling a strong compulsion** to speed ahead and cross the finish line first. At the end of the race it had been she and T.R. Peters, and they had paused just before the finish line, balancing motionless on their bicycles. The time had seemed endless, and then T.R. lost his balance and his foot touched the ground and Sara was the winner.

She slipped on some dry leaves, went down on her knees, straightened, and paused to catch her breath.

"Are you all right?"

"Yes, I just slipped."

She waited for a moment, bent over her knees, then she called, "Charlie! Charlie," without lifting her head.

"Oh, Charleeeeee," Joe shouted above her.

Sara knew Charlie would shout back if he heard her, the long wailing cry he gave sometimes when he was frightened during the night. It was such a familiar cry that for a moment she thought she heard it.

....

Her progress up the hill seemed It seemed like she was walking up the hill

all the while feeling a strong compulsion when she really wanted

She waited, still touching the ground with one hand, until she was sure there was no answer.

"Come on," Joe said, holding out his hand.

He **pulled her to her feet** and she stood looking up at the top of the hill. Machines had cut away the earth there to get at the veins of coal, and the earth had been pushed down the hill to form a **huge bank**.

"I'll never get up that," she said. She leaned against a tree whose leaves were covered with the pale fine dirt which had filtered down when the machines had cut away the hill.

"**Sure you will.** I've been up it a dozen times."

He took her hand and she **started after** him, moving sideways up the steep bank. The dirt crumbled beneath her feet and she slid, skinned one knee, and then slipped again. When she had regained her balance she laughed wryly and said, "What's going to happen is that I'll end up pulling you all the way down the hill."

"No, I've got you. Keep coming."

She started again, putting one foot carefully above the other, picking her way over the stones. When she paused,

....

pulled her to her feet helped her stand up
huge bank big hill of dirt
Sure you will. Yes, you can.
started after followed

he said, "Keep coming. We're almost there."

"I think **it's a trick**, like at the dentist's when he says, 'I'm almost through drilling.' Then he drills for another hour and says, 'Now, I'm really almost through drilling,' and he keeps on and then says, 'There's just one more spot and then I'll be practically really through.'"

"We must go to the same dentist."

"I don't think I can make it. There's no skin at all left on the sides of my legs."

"Well, we're really almost practically there now, in the words of your dentist."

She fell across the top of the dirt bank on her stomach, rested for a moment, and then turned and looked down the valley.

....

it's a trick you are just saying that to make me go farther

BEFORE YOU MOVE ON...

1. **Setting** Reread page 118. Describe where Charlie was. Why was it hard for others to find him there?

2. **Cause and Effect** How did Sara climb to the top of the hill? How was this experience different from other experiences that summer?

LOOK AHEAD Read pages 128–142 to find out how Sara changes as she looks for Charlie.

At the top of the hill, Sara and Joe call out Charlie's name over and over again. Sara thinks she hears Charlie.

Chapter Nineteen

She could not speak for a moment. There lay the whole valley in a way she had never imagined it, a **tiny finger of civilization set in a sweeping expanse of dark forest**. The black treetops seemed **to crowd against** the yards, the houses, the roads, **giving the impression that at any moment** the trees would close over the houses like waves and leave nothing but an unbroken line of black-green leaves waving in the sunlight.

Up the valley she could see the intersection where they shopped, the drugstore, the gas station where her mother had once won a set of twenty-four stemmed glasses which Aunt Willie would not allow them to use, the grocery store, the lot where the yellow school buses were parked

....

tiny finger of civilization set in a sweeping expanse of dark forest small town in the center of a large forest

to crowd against so close to

giving the impression that at any moment so that it looked like

for the summer. She could look over the valley and see another hill where white cows were all grouped together by a fence and beyond that another hill and then another.

She looked back at the valley and she saw the lake and for the first time since she had stood up on the hill she remembered Charlie.

Raising her hand to her mouth, she called, "Charlie! Charlie! Charlie!" There was a faint echo that seemed to waver in her ears.

"Charlie, oh, Charlie!" Her voice was so loud it seemed to ram into the valley.

Sara waited. She looked down at the forest, and everything was so quiet it seemed to her that the whole valley, the whole world was waiting with her.

"Charlie, hey, Charlie!" Joe shouted.

"Charleeeeee!" She made the sound of it last a long time. "Can you hear meeeeee?"

With her eyes she followed the trail she knew he must have taken—the house, the Akers' vacant lot, the old pasture, the forest. The forest that seemed powerful enough to **engulf a whole** valley, she thought with a sinking feeling, could certainly swallow up a young boy.

....

engulf a whole swallow the entire

"Charlie! Charlie! Charlie!" There was a waver in the last syllable that **betrayed how near she was to tears**. She looked down at the Indian slipper she was still holding.

"Charlie, oh, Charlie." She waited. There was not a sound anywhere. "Charlie, where are you?"

"Hey, Charlie!" Joe shouted.

They waited in the same dense silence. A cloud passed in front of the sun and a breeze began to blow through the trees. Then there was silence again.

"Charlie, Charlie, Charlie, Charlie, Charlie."

She paused, listened, then bent abruptly and put Charlie's slipper to her eyes. She waited for the hot tears that had come so often this summer, the tears that had seemed so close only a moment before. Now her eyes remained dry.

I have **cried over myself** a hundred times this summer, she thought, I have wept over my big feet and my skinny legs and my nose, I have even cried over my stupid shoes, and now when I **have a true sadness** there are no tears left.

She held the felt side of the slipper against her eyes

....

betrayed how near she was to tears showed how much she wanted to cry

cried over myself cried about my own problems

have a true sadness really have something to cry about; am really sad

like a blindfold and stood there, feeling the hot sun on her head and the wind wrapping around her legs, conscious of the height and the valley sweeping down from her feet.

"Listen, just because you can't hear him doesn't mean anything. He could be—"

"Wait a minute." She lowered the slipper and looked down the valley. A sudden wind blew dust into her face and she lifted her hand to shield her eyes.

"I thought I heard something. Charlie! Answer me right this minute."

She waited with the slipper held against her breasts, one hand to her eyes, her whole body motionless, concentrating on her brother. Then she stiffened. She thought again she had heard something—Charlie's long high wail. Charlie could sound sadder than anyone when he cried.

In her anxiety she took the slipper and twisted it again and again as if she were wringing water out. She called, then stopped abruptly and listened. She looked at Joe and he shook his head slowly.

She looked away. A bird rose from the trees below and

In her anxiety Feeling worried and scared,

flew toward the hills in the distance. She waited **until she could see it no longer** and then slowly, still listening for the call that didn't come, she sank to the ground and sat with her head bent over her knees.

Beside her, Joe scuffed his foot in the dust and sent a cascade of rocks and dirt down the bank. When the sound of it faded, he began to call, "Charlie, hey, Charlie," again and again.

----

until she could see it no longer until she couldn't see it anymore

Charlie wakes up feeling sad, tired, and scared.
Then he hears someone call his name.

Chapter Twenty

Charlie awoke, but he lay for a moment without opening his eyes. He did not remember where he was, but he **had a certain dread of seeing it.**

There were **great parts of his life that were lost to Charlie,** blank spaces that he could never fill in. He would find himself in a strange place and not know how he had got there. Like the time Sara had been hit in the nose with a baseball at the Dairy Queen, and the blood and the sight of Sara kneeling on the ground in helpless pain had frightened him so much that he had turned and run **without direction,** in a frenzy, dashing headlong up the street, blind to cars and people.

By chance Mr. Weicek had seen him, put him in the car, and driven him home, and Aunt Willie had put him

....

had a certain dread of seeing it was scared to open his eyes and see where he was

great parts of his life that were lost to Charlie parts of Charlie's life that he could not remember

without direction not knowing where he was going

to bed, but later he remembered none of this. He had only awakened in bed and looked at the crumpled bit of ice cream cone still clenched in his hand and wondered about it.

His whole life **had been built on a strict routine**, and as long as this routine was kept up, he felt safe and well. The same foods, the same bed, the same furniture in the same place, the same seat on the school bus, the same class procedure were all important to him. But always there could be **the unexpected, the dreadful surprise that would topple his carefully constructed life in an instant**.

The first thing he became aware of was the twigs pressing into his face, and he put his hand under his cheek. Still he did not open his eyes. Pictures began to drift into his mind; he saw Aunt Willie's cigar box which was filled with old jewelry and buttons and knickknacks, and he found that he could remember every item in that box—the string of white beads without a clasp, the old earrings, the tiny book with souvenir fold-out pictures of New York, the plastic decorations from cakes, the turtle made of sea shells. Every item was so real that he opened his eyes and was surprised to see, instead of the glittering

....

had been built on a strict routine was the same every day
**the unexpected, the dreadful surprise that would topple
his carefully constructed life in an instant** something new
that would change his happy life

contents of the box, the dull and unfamiliar forest.

He raised his head and immediately felt the aching of his body. Slowly he sat up and looked down at his hands. His fingernails were black with earth, two of them broken below the quick, and he got up slowly and sat on the log behind him and **inspected** his fingers more closely.

Then he sat up straight. His hands dropped to his lap. **His head cocked to the side** like a bird listening. Slowly he straightened until he was standing. At his side his fingers twitched at the empty air as if to grasp something. He took a step forward, still with his head to the side. He remained absolutely still.

Then he began to cry out in a hoarse excited voice, again and again, screaming now, because he had just heard someone far away calling his name.

....

inspected looked at

His head cocked to the side He turned his head

Sara hears a familiar cry. Have they found Charlie at last?

Chapter Twenty–One

At the top of the hill Sara got slowly to her feet and stood looking down at the forest. She pushed the hair back from her forehead and moistened her lips. The wind dried them as she waited.

Joe started to say something but she reached out one hand and took his arm to stop him. **Scarcely daring to believe her ears**, she stepped closer to the edge of the bank. Now she heard it **unmistakably**—the sharp repeated cry—and she knew it was Charlie.

"Charlie!" she shouted with all her might.

She paused and listened, and his cries were louder and she knew he was not far away after all, just down the slope, in the direction of the ravine.

"It's Charlie, it's Charlie!"

A wild joy overtook her and she jumped up and down

....

Scarcely daring to believe her ears Not believing what she heard

unmistakably and she knew she was right this time

on the bare earth and she felt that she could crush the whole hill just by jumping if she wanted.

She sat and scooted down the bank, sending earth and pebbles in a cascade before her. She landed on the soft ground, ran a few steps, lost her balance, caught hold of the first tree trunk she could find, and swung around till she stopped.

She let out another whoop of pure joy, turned and ran down the hill in great strides, the puce tennis shoes slapping the ground like rubber paddles, the wind in her face, her hands grabbing one tree trunk after another for support. She felt like a wild creature who had traveled through the forest this way for a lifetime. Nothing could stop her now.

At the edge of the ravine she paused and stood gasping for breath. Her heart was beating so fast **it pounded** in her ears, and her throat was dry. She leaned against a tree, resting her cheek against the rough bark.

She thought for a minute she was going to faint, a thing she had never done before, not even when she broke her nose. She hadn't even believed people really did faint until this minute when she clung to the tree because her

---

it pounded she could hear it

legs were as useless as rubber bands.

There was a ringing in her ears and another sound, **a wailing siren-like cry that was painfully familiar.**

"Charlie?"

Charlie's crying, like the sound of a cricket, seemed everywhere and nowhere.

She walked along the edge of the ravine, circling the large boulders and trees. Then she looked down into the ravine where the shadows lay, and she felt as if something had turned over inside her because she saw Charlie.

He was standing in his torn pajamas, face turned upward, hands raised, shouting **with all his might**. His eyes were shut tight. His face was streaked with dirt and tears. His pajama jacket hung in shreds about his scratched chest.

He opened his eyes and as he saw Sara a strange expression **came over** his face, an expression of wonder and joy and disbelief, and Sara knew that if she lived to be a hundred no one would ever look at her quite that way again.

She paused, looked down at him, and then, sliding on the seat of her pants, went down the bank and took him

....

a wailing siren-like cry that was painfully familiar
a loud, sad cry that she had heard many times before

with all his might as loud as he could

came over showed on

in her arms.

"Oh, Charlie."

His arms gripped her like steel.

"Oh, Charlie."

She could feel his fingers digging into her back as he clutched her shirt. "It's all right now, Charlie, I'm here and we're going home." His face was buried in her shirt and she patted his head, and said again, "It's all right now. Everything's fine."

She held him against her for a moment and now the hot tears were in her eyes and on her cheeks and she didn't even notice.

"I know how you feel," she said. "I know. One time when I had the measles and my fever was real high, I got lost on my way back from the bathroom, right in our house, and it was a terrible feeling, terrible, because I wanted to get back to my bed and I couldn't find it, and finally Aunt Willie heard me and came and you know where I was? In the kitchen. In our kitchen and I couldn't have been more lost if I'd been out in the middle of the wilderness."

She patted the back of his head again and said, "Look,

··

His arms gripped her like steel. He hugged her tightly.

I even brought your bedroom slipper. **Isn't that service, huh?**"

She tried to show it to him, but he was still clutching her, and she held him against her, patting him. After a moment she said again, "Look, here's your slipper. Let's put it on." She knelt, put his foot into the shoe, and said, "Now, isn't that better?"

He nodded slowly, **his chest still heaving with unspent sobs**.

"Can you walk home?"

He nodded. She took **her shirttail** and wiped his tears and smiled at him. "Come on, we'll find a way out of here and go home."

"Hey, over this way," Joe called from the bank of the ravine. Sara had forgotten about him in the excitement of finding Charlie, and she looked up at him for a moment.

"Over this way, around the big tree," Joe called. "That's probably how he got in. The rest of the ravine is a mass of brier bushes."

She put one arm around Charlie and led him around the tree. "Everybody in town's looking for you, you know that?" she said. "Everybody. The police came and all

....

Isn't that service, huh? I'm a great helper.

his chest still heaving with unspent sobs and he was breathing heavily because he wanted to cry

her shirttail the bottom of her shirt

the neighbors are out—there must be a hundred people looking for you. **You were on the radio. It's like you were the President of the United States or something.** Everybody was saying, 'Where's Charlie?' and 'We got to find Charlie.'"

Suddenly Charlie stopped and held up his hand and Sara looked down. "What is it?"

He pointed to the silent watch.

She smiled. "Charlie, you are something, you know that? Here we are racing down the hill to tell everyone in great triumph that you are found, *found*, and we have to stop and wind your watch first."

She looked at the watch, saw that the stem was missing, and shook her head. "It's broken, Charlie, see, the stem's gone. It's broken."

He held it out again.

"It's *broken*, Charlie. We'll have to take it to the jeweler and have it fixed."

He continued to hold out his arm.

"Hey, Charlie, you want to wear my watch till you get yours fixed?" Joe asked. He slid down the bank and put his watch on Charlie's arm. "There."

....

You were on the radio. It's like you were the President of the United States or something. People heard about you on the radio like you were a very important person.

Charlie **bent his face close** and listened.

"Now can we go home?" Sara asked, jamming her hands into her back pockets.

Charlie nodded.

....

bent his face close leaned down to the watch

BEFORE YOU MOVE ON...

1. **Comparisons** In the past, Sara was impatient and annoyed with Charlie. How did she act when she found him? What caused this change?

2. **Author's Style** Reread pages 136–137. What words show how happy Sara was?

LOOK AHEAD Read pages 143–154 to find out what Sara wants to show Charlie.

Sara and Joe bring Charlie home. The swans fly over the town as everyone comes to greet Charlie.

Chapter Twenty–Two

They walked through the woods for a long time, Joe in the lead, picking the best path, with Charlie and Sara following. **From time to time** Sara turned and hugged Charlie and he smelled of trees and dark earth and tears and she said, "Everybody's going to be so glad to see you it's going to be **just like New Year's Eve**."

Sara could not understand why she suddenly felt so good. **It was a puzzle.** The day before she had been miserable. She had wanted to fly away from everything, like the swans to a new lake, and now she didn't want that any more.

Down the hill Mr. Rhodes, one of the searchers, was coming toward them and Joe called out, "Mr. Rhodes, Sara found him!"

"Is he all right?" Mr. Rhodes called back.

....

From time to time Every few minutes
just like New Year's Eve like a big party
It was a puzzle. She didn't understand it.

"Fine, he's fine."

"Sara found him and he's all right. He's all right." **The phrase passed down the hill** from Dusty Rhodes, who painted cars at the garage, to Mr. Aker to someone Sara couldn't recognize.

Then all the searchers were joining them, reaching out to pat Charlie and to say to Sara, "Oh, your aunt is going to be so happy," or "Where *was* he?" or "Well, now we can all sleep in peace tonight."

They came through the woods in a big noisy group and out into the late sunlight in the old pasture, Sara and Charlie in the middle, surrounded by all the searchers.

Suddenly Sara sensed a movement above her. She looked up and then grabbed Charlie's arm.

The swans were directly overhead, flying with outstretched necks, their long wings beating the air, **an awkward blind sort of flight**. They were so low that she thought they might hit the trees, but at the last moment they **pulled up** and skimmed the air just above the treetops.

"Look, Charlie, look. Those are the swans. Remember?

....

The phrase passed down the hill People told their friends the good news about Charlie

an awkward blind sort of flight they flew in a strange way, like they couldn't see

pulled up started to fly higher

They're going home."

He looked blankly at the sky, unable to associate the heavy awkward birds with the graceful swans he had seen on the water. He squinted at the sky, then looked at Sara, puzzled.

"Charlie, those are the swans. Remember? At the lake?" she said, looking right at him. "They're going home now. Don't you remember? They were—"

"Hey, there's your aunt, Charlie. There's Aunt Willie coming."

Sara was still pulling at Charlie's arm, directing his attention to the sky. It seemed **urgent** somehow that Charlie see the swans once again. She said, "Charlie, those are—"

He looked instead across the field and he broke away from Sara and started running. She took two steps after him and then stopped. Aunt Willie in her bright green dress seemed to shine like a **beacon**, and he hurried toward her, an awkward figure in torn blue pajamas, shuffling through the high grass.

There was a joyous yell that was so shrill Sara thought it had come from the swans, but then she knew that it had

....

urgent important
beacon bright light

come from Charlie, for the swans were mute.

"Here he is, Willie," Mrs. Aker called, running behind Charlie to have some part in the reunion.

Aunt Willie was coming as fast as she could on her bad legs. "I never thought to see him again," she was telling everyone and no one. "I thought he was up in that mine. I tell you, I never thought to see him again. Charlie, come here to your Aunt Willie."

Charlie ran like a ball rolling downhill, bouncing with the slope of the land.

"I tell you this has been **the blackest day** of my life"— Aunt Willie was gasping—"and I include every day I have been on earth. Charlie, my Charlie, let me look at you. Oh, **you are a sight**."

He fell into Aunt Willie's arms. Over his head Aunt Willie said through her tears to Mrs. Aker, "**May you never lose your Bobby**, that's all I got to say. May you never lose your Bobby, may none of you ever lose anybody in the woods or in the mine or anywhere."

Sara stood in the pasture by the old gray shack and watched the swans disappear over the hill, and then she watched Charlie and Aunt Willie disappear in the crowd

....

the blackest day the worst day

you are a sight I am so happy to see you

May you never lose your Bobby I hope your son never gets lost

of people, and she felt good and loose and she thought that if she started walking down the hill at that moment, she would walk with the light movements of a puppet and never touch the ground at all.

She thought she would sit down for a moment now that everyone was gone, but when she looked around she saw Joe Melby still standing behind her. "I thought you went with the others."

"Nope."

"It's been a very strange day for me." She looked at the horizon where the swans had disappeared.

"It's been one of my stranger days, too."

"Well, I'd better go home."

Joe walked a few steps with her, cleared his throat, and then said, "Do you want to go to Bennie Hoffman's party with me?"

She thought **she hadn't heard him right for a moment,** or if she had, that it was a mistake, like the boy who shouted, "Hey, beautiful," at Rosey Camdon.

"What?"

"I asked if you wanted to go with me to the party."

"I wasn't invited." She made herself think of the swans. By this time they could probably see the lake at

....

she hadn't heard him right for a moment she heard the wrong thing

the university and were about to settle down on the water with a great beating of wings and ruffling of feathers. She could almost see the long perfect glide that would bring them to the water.

"I'm inviting you. Bennie said I could bring somebody if I wanted to. He begged me to bring someone, as a matter of fact. He and Sammy and John and Pete have formed this musical group and they're going to make everybody listen to them."

"Well, I don't know."

"Why not? Other than the fact that you're going to have to listen to some terrible guitar playing. Bennie Hoffman has had about one and a half lessons."

"Well . . ."

"**It's not any big deal**, just sitting in Bennie Hoffman's back yard and watching him **louse up** with a two-hundred-dollar guitar and amplifier."

"I guess I could go."

"I'll walk over and **pick you up** in half an hour. It won't matter if we're late. The last fifty songs will sound about the same as the first fifty."

"I'll be ready."

....

It's not any big deal It's not important
louse up make mistakes
pick you up come find you

148

Sara's father calls at last. Sara starts to think
about her life in a new way.

Chapter Twenty–Three

When Sara came up the walk Wanda was standing on the porch. "What is going on around here, will you tell me that? Where is Charlie?"

"We found him. He's with Aunt Willie, wherever that is."

"Do you know how I heard he was lost? I heard it on the car radio when I was coming home. How do you think that made me feel—to hear **from some disc jockey** that my own brother was missing? I could hardly get here because there are a hundred cars full of people jamming the street down there."

"Well, he's fine."

"**So Mr. Aker told me, only** I would like to see him and find out what happened."

....

from some disc jockey on the radio
So Mr. Aker told me, only That's what Mr. Aker said, but

"He got up during the night sometime—this is what I think happened—to go see the swans and ended up in a ravine crying his heart out."

Wanda stepped off the porch and looked across the street, leaning to see around the foliage by the fence. She said, "Is that them over there on the Carsons' porch?"

Sara looked and nodded.

"Honestly, Charlie still in his pajamas, and Aunt Willie in her good green dress with a handkerchief tied around her forehead to keep her from sweating, and both of them eating watermelon. **That beats all.**"

"At least he's all right."

Wanda started down the walk, then paused. "You want to come?"

"No, I'm going to a party."

"Whose?"

"Bennie Hoffman's."

"I didn't think you were invited."

"Joe Melby's taking me."

"Joe Melby? Your great and terrible enemy?"

"He is not my enemy, Wanda. He is one of the nicest people I know."

....

That beats all. That is so strange.

"For three months I've been hearing about **the evils of Joe Melby**. Joe Melby, the thief; Joe Melby, the fink; Joe Melby, the—"

"A person," Sara said coldly, "**can occasionally be mistaken**." She turned and went into the living room, saw Boysie sleeping by the door and said, "Boysie, we found Charlie." She bent and rubbed him behind the ears. Then she went into the kitchen, made a sandwich, and was starting into the bedroom when the phone rang.

"Hello," she said, her mouth full of food.

"Hello, I have a long-distance call for Miss Willamina Godfrey," the operator said.

"Oh, she's across the street. If you'll wait a minute I'll go get her."

"Operator, I'll just talk to whoever's there," Sara heard her father say.

She said quickly, "No, I'll go get her. Just wait one minute. It won't take any time. She's right across the street."

"Sara? Is this Sara?"

"Yes, this is me." The strange feeling came over her

....

the evils of Joe Melby what a bad person Joe Melby is
can occasionally be mistaken can be wrong sometimes

again. "If you wait a minute I'll go get Aunt Willie."

"Sara, did you find Charlie?"

"Yes, we found him, but I don't mind going to get Aunt Willie. They're over on the Carsons' porch."

"Is Charlie all right?"

"He's fine. He's eating watermelon right now."

"Where was he?"

"Well, he went up into the woods and got lost. We found him in a ravine and he was dirty and tired and hungry but he's all right."

"That's good. I was going to come home tonight if he hadn't been found."

"Oh."

"But since everything's all right, I guess I'll just wait until the weekend."

"Sure."

"So I'll probably see you Saturday, then, **if nothing turns up**."

"Fine."

"Be sure to tell Willie I called."

"I will."

....

if nothing turns up unless something happens that is more important

A picture came into her mind of the laughing, curly-headed man with the broken tooth in the photograph album, and she suddenly saw life as **a series** of huge, uneven steps, and she saw herself on the steps, standing motionless in her prison shirt, and she had just taken an enormous step up out of the shadows, and she was standing, waiting, and there were other steps in front of her, so that she could go as high as the sky, and she saw Charlie on **a flight of** small difficult steps, and her father down at the bottom of some steps, just sitting and not trying to go further. She saw everyone she knew on those blinding white steps and for a moment everything was clearer than it had ever been.

"Sara?"

"I'm still here."

"Well, that was all I wanted, just to hear that Charlie was all right."

"He's fine."

"And I'll see you on Saturday if nothing happens."

"Sure."

"Good-by."

....

a series a lot

a flight of a set of

She sat for a minute still holding the receiver and then she set it back on the telephone and finished her sandwich. Slowly she **slipped off** her tennis shoes and looked down at her feet, which were dyed blue. Then she got up quickly and went to get ready for the party.

....

slipped off took off; removed

BEFORE YOU MOVE ON...

1. **Inference** Reread page 145. Why was it so important for Sara to tell Charlie about the swans flying above them?

2. **Summarize** Reread page 153. Describe the steps in Sara's thoughts. What did the steps mean to Sara?